Keeping the Night Watch

Fred Johnston

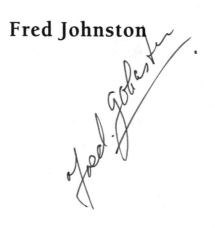

THE COLLINS PRESS

Published by The Collins Press, Carey's Lane, The Huguenot Quarter, Cork 1998

Published with the assistance of the Arts Council/An Chomhairle Ealaíonn

The Arts Council
An Chomhairle Ealaíon

Acknowledgements are due to the following publications in which some of these stories first appeared: *Stand*, *The London Magazine*, *The North Dakota Quarterly*, *The Antigonish Review*, *New Irish Writing* (*The Sunday Tribune*), *The Cream City Review* (USA). Acknowledgement is also due to Crazy Cow Music for the use of the lines from the Joni Mitchell song 'Canada'. Particular thanks are due to Una Sinnott and Marguerite Morley for their invaluable assistance in preparing the manuscripts.

British Library Cataloguing in Publication data.

Printed in Ireland by Sci Print, Shannon

Front cover painting reproduced by permission of the artist, Gleigh Gaughan

Typesetting by Red Barn Publishing, Skeagh, Skibbereen, Co. Cork

Jacket design by Upper Case Ltd., Cornmarket Street, Cork

ISBN: 1-898256-58-6

Contents

Then at other times other people confirmed and completed the story: till it stood at last before me, a tale formidable and simple, as they always are, those disclosures of obscure trials endured by ignorant hearts.

—Joseph Conrad, 'The Idiots'

For Sylvia

Safe Harbour

She turned her face, eyes closed, to the sun.

A world moved contentedly behind her eyelids. She imagined vague pleasures and wallowed in their milky spin and drift. On days like this, a magical simplicity infected everything. She sat in the hot car, one door open, her left leg lazing out of the car, her sandal grazing the gravel surface of the small promenade. She had her colourful flower-patterned skirt pulled up around her knees, a gesture which gave her immense but indefinable pleasure. She felt the light warm breeze travel excitedly along her thighs, cool over the sweat between her legs. The radio was on, some very bad Irish Country 'n' Western music. The waltzy beat threaded out appallingly gushy sentiments of exile, heartbreak and lost mother-love. The world belonged to her. It began with her in the car and it radiated outwards from that point. On days like these she became a tiny sun.

The river was calm today, a murky mirror spotted here and there with fat lazy swans and the hysterical dash and cackle of duck and waterhen. High reeds shook under the kiss of the breeze. The sounds of children floated over the water, mixed in with the sluggish chug-chug of a boat's engine. The children would have spotted the car, would be waving enthusiastically, *Look at me, Mammy, Look at me, Mammy,* and she would as usual tantalise them by appearing to take no notice of them. She smiled, keeping her eyes closed. There were times when her contentment bordered on boredom. She had nothing in the world to bother her. Was she lucky, as friends now and then implied? Perhaps luck had something to do with it. Others might climb the Himalayas, take broken-down hippy lovers, ride the Trans-Siberian Express, work on a kibbutz. None of that sort of thing had ever been for her; here, some faces and names drifted behind her closed eyelids. Raising children was adventure enough. Keeping a home. The prospect of these things had always excited her. They excited her still. There was a satisfying old-fashioned sense of building something. She enjoyed old virtues, ideas, books, furniture. She had never expressed a wish to holiday in, say, the United States, which was a new country; no, she always opted for old countries, like Spain and Greece. Old-fashioned things were comforting.

The boat was coming closer. She opened her eyes, inspected herself quickly in the rear-view mirror, saw there a late-thirtyish face carefully bronzed, good bright eyes, a thin but firm mouth, and skin that hadn't betrayed her so far. A wrinkle here and there simply added character. Her light blonde hair was still thick and shiny. Walking with the children through town, she was aware of young men's stares. Her figure was damned good. Admiring and lustful looks made her feel sexy. Life was good.

The boat glided in with a soft bump against the worn tractor tyres hung over the edge of the quay wall. It was a small boat with a tiny cabin at the front, a sort of converted lobster boat, useful for Sunday afternoon outings on the river and some occasional fishing. Richard had converted it – well, that was his word. He'd repainted it, as far as she could tell, replaced the ancient engine, nailed in one or two seats. That was about all. She had parked the car deliberately at an angle to where the boat would be berthed, which would allow her husband an uninterrupted view, when he raised his head, all the way up her brown right leg, just about as far as he'd want to look. It was a game with them. They would drive quickly back to the house, park the children in the back garden, then pretend there was something to do in the car. They'd drive it down the long, curved driveway out of sight of the house and, in stifling heat and with all the windows closed, they'd bite, scratch, tear at each other's clothing until neither could stand it and she'd mount her husband over the front passenger seat and jam her fingers in his mouth when he cried out. Someday the children might catch them. But, although she shuddered to admit it, there was an added excitement in their nearness and the risk of being caught.

She was lucky, of course she was. Ten years of marriage hadn't quelled their sexual ardour or, for that matter, their inventiveness. Richard was good to look at, broad-shouldered, tanned, clean-shaven, a stroke or two of regal grey at his temples. Women admired him, she was sure of it. She was also sure he was aware of their admiration. They were both very sexual creatures. Sex involved tenderness, savagery, greed, murmurings, shouting. They could have had oceans of children. But, sensibly, they had settled for two. Richard, like all men, had wanted a son. She'd fallen down in that area. Fiona and Cliona were beautiful children, though, you had to admit. Blondes, both of them. Blue-eyed, and so charming. An old-fashioned word, charming. But old-fashioned was so comforting.

Richard helped the two girls out of the boat. Fiona, she reflected, would arrive at puberty first. She was a little taller than her sister and had a more argumentative nature. She took after Richard and would have his ambition. Cliona was dreamier, wider-faced, more imaginative. Neither girl had ever shown much interest in playing with dolls. They looked fat and comical now, snugly enclosed in their bright orange life-jackets.

She leaned behind her and opened the back door. Richard shouted for them to take off their jackets and leave them in the boat. The two jackets sailed through the air and Richard danced about trying to catch them. Everyone laughed. Richard secured his boat, which he had christened *Julie's Folly* after what he referred to as her 'folly' at marrying a humdrum, day-to-day, middle-management type like himself when *you could have any man in this town*. Well, she hadn't wanted just any man, she'd wanted him. She had recognised his gift for security and order – these things were a gift – and had been attracted to him almost at once. Her earlier love affairs had been all fun and chaos. Even thinking about that life made her shiver. Was it so terrible that one took time to fall in love, that love itself was not the main motive for marrying someone? Well, of course, it *should* be, almost always. It was the one old-fashioned ideal that she had not been quite able to live up to. But she forgave herself easily. She had, after all, managed to love Richard in time. Now she loved him, and that cancelled out everything else. And he wasn't middle-management any more. He was top management. You couldn't help admiring his determination and patience. To stay in what was once a small-town, one-big-window advertising agency and encourage and develop that agency until it became one of the largest in the country, with all the ruthlessness that such development entailed, was a great achievement. How many men would have managed it? Not that many. You had to admire Richard; you *had* to.

The house waited for them at the top of the winding gravel driveway, its windows gleaming in the setting sun. Their black labrador, Silk, leaped up at the slowing vehicle, her tongue hanging out wetly, her throat loaded with deep, contented growls. The sun sparkled and ran in rivers along the dog's groomed coat. Fiona and Cliona rapped the car windows, delighted as always to have Silk jumping up at them. Richard smelled faintly of engine oil and salt. His presence beside her was like a warm fire on a windy, wet night. She brought the car to a dignified stop at the big mock-Georgian front door. Everyone got out with a rush. Silk had to be restrained from coming into the house; all those thick black hairs on the carpet, the furniture. The big brass door knocker shaped like a lion's head felt heavy and solid under her push. The smell of the house; that fabulously reassuring familiarity, a mix of air-freshener, polish and cooking, swept over her. She was the first in. She led her family after her. She would get tea ready and take care of Richard's libido later. The sun would be up for some time yet. They would, as usual, invent something wrong with the car.

But after tea a happy lassitude crept over her, and she found herself a comfortable position in a window-seat and dozed off. When she woke up, Fiona and Cliona were busying themselves over homework at the end of the lounge. Down the stairs came the rhythmic tapping of Richard's fingers on the keys of his word processor. She eased herself out of the big soft chair. The children didn't look up. She tip-toed upstairs, opened the door of his study. He was hunched over the machine, his head moving from the screen to a neat pile of typed sheets at his side. She crept up on him, slipped her arms around his neck. He sighed, kept typing. No, she said, as huskily as she could manage. Let your fingers do the walking down *here*. She placed the fingers of his left hand on her mound. The warmth invaded her, a slow, steady, upwards rush. He turned round to her, swivelling in his chair. He muttered something she couldn't make out, then kissed her hard between her legs. Even through the material of her skirt the effect was excruciating. Her knees gave way. You pick the oddest times, Richard said. But she heard in his voice that magic catch of emotion and she knew she had him.

He lifted her skirt, rubbed his mouth hard over her crotch, pulled down her panties and used his mouth all over her. She was pulling him by the hair now. He stood up, pushed her back against the wall. She opened his trousers, felt how enormous he'd grown, felt herself powerful and strong, opened her legs and let him insert himself, with her hand guiding and kneading. The heat and pleasure grew. She moved with him, her back scraping against the wall. She murmured for a while, then couldn't restrain herself and sang out over his shoulder. He pushed harder and harder and let himself go, his head flung back, his knees buckling, his fingers pressed deep in the flesh of her buttocks. He relaxed with great exhalations of breath. His face was covered in sweat. When he pulled out of her, cool air drifted over her wet thighs. Downstairs, Cliona was shouting for her.

She pulled up her panties, heard Richard turning on the shower as she went downstairs. I can do all this, she told herself. I can make miracles happen in my own house every day of the week. As she descended the stairs, she understood how it must be to go down a flight of stairs into a regal ball. All that restrained power; no wonder the guests applauded. Cliona and Fiona were arguing over the allocation of coloured pencils. As she walked towards them, she picked up the carelessly-opened pages of Sunday newspapers. Scandals in the business world, investigations. Well, Richard had done well to stay in a small town, where none of these things happened. If they did, you didn't read about them in the newspapers. The growth of the town had been accompanied by the establishment of a certain type of order. People knew where they stood. They had both been born and raised in this town. They had *certain rights*. One heard things now and then, but, if the local press ever did, they too knew their place. The newspapers carried photographs of prominent politicians over captions questioning this decision and that. It was all so wearisome. She bundled the pages up and carried them out to the bin in the kitchen. Cliona followed her, wet-eyed.

Don't let her tell lies, Mammy, Fiona shouted cautiously from the lounge. I'm not telling lies, Cliona sniffled. She crouched down and wiped the tears from Cliona's face. They're *my* colours, her daughter said. Liar! shouted Fiona. You will not call your sister a liar, Julie ordered. You will say you're sorry. I'm not sorry, called Fiona. You are, said her mother.

Night. It came down over the river and the house like a blanket. Stars pierced the night sky. A sickle moon climbed heavily out of the water. She lay in bed, staring at the ceiling. The big bedroom windows were open and she could hear the very distant sounds of cars, a voice, an aircraft landing at the small airport nearby. For some odd reason, she was rarely able to get what one might describe as a good night's sleep. Her heart pounded too loudly, her eyelids refused to stay closed. She was always curiously excited at night. Most times she would get out of bed and go downstairs, making sure not to disturb Richard, and make some tea. Tonight seemed to call for a valium. She unwound herself from the bedclothes and went downstairs.

The kitchen light, when she switched it on, blinded her for a moment. She stood there, dressed only in bra and panties, and looked around her. The kitchen seemed cold, the black windows threatening. She found the valium, washed one down with a glass of water, closed her eyes, then walked slowly back into the lounge.

Lulled by the drug, she allowed herself to look out through the big front windows, over the dark sloping lawn, over the trees, down to the river and then up to the lights of the town in the distance, a reddish glow at the foot of the sky. The darkness of the night was both comforting and menacing. It seemed to suck her outwards through the glass. Nothing moved out there, there wasn't the slightest breeze to filter through the branches of the trees down by the road. To her left, a mile or so away, the black hulk of a ruined castle leaned against the curtain of stars and sky. Did it have a ghost? Some locals said it did. The Black-and-Tans had imprisoned and tortured a young man there, chained him to a wall and allowed him to starve to death. His ghost could be heard crying, it was rumoured, on certain dark nights. Another *pishogue*, a superstition, the sort of thing that clouded the Irish psyche and, for all anyone knew, coloured our reaction to the twentieth century. She smiled to herself, saw her own face smiling back in the glass of the window. She had no such fear of ghosts or ghouls. She had been born into a generation that had embraced enlightenment. It didn't bother her that the changes in Irish life whose benefits she enjoyed had been fought for by other, more adventurous women. She was a *new woman*. Not at all like her mother or her grandmother, priest-fearing, guilt-ridden. They believed in ghosts, of course. Not her. And not her daughters, either. She'd seen to that. But she had sent them both to an Irish-speaking infants' school. She wanted them to have culture of some sort, at least to be wholly Irish. *New* Irish, that is; let there be no mistake. To know that to be an Irish woman was not to be second class in any way.

Full to the brim with calm thoughts about politics and their daughters' future, she peered into the darkness, saw only her own peering reflection. Not so much as a breath to rustle the leaves on the trees down by the road. Everyone who was anyone spoke Irish these days, she reflected. Her command of the language of her grandmother was rusty. That wouldn't do. She would scour the local papers, sign on at an evening class. It would give her something to do. Not that she wasn't satisfied with what she had to do already. She shivered. All that darkness out there, and not a breath. One could walk out of the front door, down the garden, and disappear, dissolve. People disappeared all the time – what were the annual figures from that TV programme? Something hideous, anyway. Just disappeared. It would do her good to learn a bit more Irish. Just walked off into the world and God only knew what happened to them.

Then, for one terrible moment, she imagined that the eyes looking back into her own were not hers, they had altered somehow, slightly, subtly, but they had changed. They were her mother's eyes. Was she becoming her mother? Was this a sign of some sort? Well, she didn't believe in that sort of thing. But she blinked, looked again, and everything was back to normal. She looked away from the window, felt her heart pound against the valium, once, twice, then it slowed down. She turned back into the darkened lounge – what if the blackness beyond the window were somehow to seep into the house, choke Richard, her daughters; herself?

The night became a treacherous and unstable place. One peered into it and it peered back. The quietness of the house reassured her. Familiar things, smells, creakings in the walls. They had built this house together, she and Richard. Bought the site, watched it being cleared, foundations dug, walls going up. They had made love in a freezing brick room on a bare concrete floor and called it their bedroom, although later it became the kitchen. Nothing could pull this house down or tear its roots from the earth.

The valium slipped through her veins. She felt comfortable, capable, ready for sleep. She went upstairs, back to bed, felt Richard's warm body curled against hers, drifted off into a drugged, dreamless sleep. As she slept, a slow fat sun squeezed its way out of the cloudy east. A new day spread itself across her sheets.

Richard was gone before she woke up. He had left a cup of well-sugared tea on the bedside table for her, and she had vague recollections of his pounding about the room getting dressed. He had leaned over, kissed her on the forehead. She'd listened to the car going off, then dozed, then heard the muttered scrabbling of her daughters in their room. The tea was cold, but she drank it all down. The day was bright, sun-heavy, full of birdsong. Richard, mischievously, had opened the bedroom curtains wide. Light was everywhere, tinting everything, shining and reflecting and blinding.

Fiona's voice, aching towards maturity, could be heard moving from the bedroom to the bathroom, a voice in which she detected her husband's determined authority under the child's peevishness. Cliona would grow up in Fiona's shadow. It was not fair. But there was nothing to be done about it. She swung herself out of bed, felt the rush of ticklish coolness under her feet from the thickly-piled bedside mat. She walked to the window and opened a section: at once cool morning air, full of grass and water smells, filled the room. Fiona was shouting something in bad Irish to her sister, an order, a command of some sort, teasing Cliona whose Irish was even worse. Julie felt an odd, displaced spasm of pride. Her daughters had some notion of who they were, where they came from. She had been adamant about instilling that. Occasionally, playfully, she called Richard by his name in Irish, Risteárd, but she could not find the Irish for her own name, Julie. She rubbed her eyes, stood up, allowed the blood to find her head, went to the dresser.

She waved at the two girls as they wobbled their way down the driveway, and she stood out a little and waved as they got into the back seat of her nearest neighbour's car, and then she waved again at the woman's frizzy blonde-haired head in the driver's seat. No one waved back. Julie was almost ready for her driving test. Richard had promised a decent secondhand car of her choice. The car would mean freedom. She looked forward to it. Buses were a bore and unreliable. She went back into the house, idled in front of the radio and morning talk show, trying to answer problem questions before the guest speaker did. People, mostly women, rang in about the most incredible things. Obviously, she told herself, they were bored, lonely housewives, left with all day to wonder about what had gone wrong, where all the dreams had disappeared to. They called in about errant adolescent daughters staying out all night, about how much education in sexual matters their children received in school, about a priest who had admitted fathering a child. They were stupid, shy women, their voices high-pitched with tension and moral indignation. They were concerned with nothing else in the whole world but sex and sexual scandal. They always managed to sicken her eventually. Julie switched off the radio, incensed at the mediocrity of her own sex.

In the absolute silence of the house, she dressed for town. A skirt that rode nicely along her thighs. A touch of make-up, a hint of scent. Nothing aggressive. She watched herself take on the form of the public woman She was good to look at and knew it. She felt powerfully and deliciously arrogant.

The sun was up, a few unemployed clouds huddled about the horizon with nothing to do, looking sheepish. Julie basked in the sun, stood in its heat at her door for a moment, smelled the grass, the salt from the river, listened to the invisible birds. She walked down the driveway – again, the feeling of descending with murderous grace an elegant, twisting staircase – and strolled casually up the country road towards the bus stop. Trees formed a speckled arch over her head. A light, warm breeze flirted in the branches. The bus stop was just outside the entrance to the local village church. As she approached it she saw a great number of parked vehicles glistening like fish in the sharp sunlight. There was laughter and talking and the sounds of excited children. She looked up towards the little white-painted church and saw a couple just married, she shy and giddy in her pink wide dress, he moustached, dark-suited, proud and silly-looking. A local photographer tried to arrange a group shot, parents and relatives half-drunk, eager to get to the reception, the young bride and groom not knowing what to do with themselves when the camera turned its attention elsewhere.

She thought she knew a face or two in the crowd. She did not want anyone to speak to her. There was an exasperating vulgarity about the whole thing – children running about, young girls with extravagant outfits that only made them look cheap, young men wearing white socks and slip-on black shoes; God, how she detested the commonality of that combination! The relatives looked overweight and debauched. Julie moved to the bus stop with her back to the proceedings, reached into her light brown, real-leather bag and took out a pair of dark sunglasses. She put them on, stared straight ahead of her across the road into a field full of grazing cows. Nothing on God's good earth would induce her to turn around and wave at anyone here. Gruff, beefy laughter tumbled over the cropped church lawns. Great black rooks cawed throatily in the crumbling ruins of a nearby monastery. Others answered from the ruined tower across the fields. The bus was late today, just to spite her. Maybe it would stop for ages and everyone would get a good gape at the wedding – it was infuriating! She didn't want anyone to see her, she didn't want to see anyone, at least not anyone here. The black wedding limousine looked utterly out of place, she thought. A pony and trap, that's the job for something like this. She thought of the voices of the women on the talk show. Open-hearted rurality didn't appeal to her. Behind the laughter and the brash playfulness lurked narrow-mindedness and embittered morality. The bus growled its way up the road. It was awful to say, of course, but the only real drawback involved in living in the country was having to be reminded about the people. To think that a sort of literature had come from people like that, people who knew nothing of the real world!

And to think that such literature had made this country famous! As the bus came nearer, she was gripped by a sort of claustrophobia. She dreaded getting on the bus, looking for a place to sit, mixing with people whom, she secretly believed, despised her. Even the dark glasses didn't seem to help. She felt herself about to to be surrounded by a rude, gossiping world in which she had no part. No part at all!

The bus moved off, faces up against the windows watching the wedding. She refused to look back. She had found a seat near the rear of the bus and, if the jolting of the vehicle and the smell of the engine disturbed her, she put up with it for the anonymity it gave her. From behind her dark glasses she glanced at the backs of heads, all those different shapes, different hairstyles, cheap tints. The sooner she passed her driving test and Richard got her a car of her own the better. Having to take a bus into town was irritating. But the sun slanted through the windows and the countryside, she had to admit, was good to look at. The road burrowed its way out of hollows and dips and leaped across the plain; she could look far to the west over stretches of brown-green bog and see ranges of blue mountains. For a while, looking out at it all, she could imagine all sorts of possibilities for herself, for Richard and the children. Possibilities far removed from this bus, the vulgarity of country weddings and country people. She saw the outskirts of the town approach and felt comforted. She understood the busy streets, the crowds, teeming cafés and restaurants, art galleries and enormous shops, everything glowing in anticipation of something else, something bigger, greater, waiting to be born. When she had her own car she would spend every day in a restaurant, gallery, a boutique, driving around with her friends, not just talking to them on the 'phone. She would take charge of herself, regain something.

This kind of thinking was, in an odd way, uncomfortable. She shook herself. She tried to make a plan for the day, the next few hours. The bus jogged along brazenly, loudly. Past housing estates, churches, shops, children dressed in ugly, baggy trousers and too-big plastic jackets. Everything had changed, become rude, uncaring. Even the new architecture seemed to suggest a particular kind of despair. Buildings were characterless, grey-fronted structures, storeys higher than the ancient buildings that surrounded them. The skyline of the town had lost its delicate medieval symmetry; and where were the sloping roofs she remembered from childhood, upon which she often imagined whole troops of angels or magical people danced and paraded and from which they watched over the citizens in the narrow streets below?

Progress always carried a price-tag. She smiled to herself. She would spend a couple of hours shopping and that would carry her nicely up to lunchtime. She had heard of a new lingerie boutique. Silks, satins. She would go there, perhaps, after she'd eaten. She looked into the narrow, crowded streets. A troop of teenage girls, children themselves, huddled around two or three baby carriages admiring the tiny bundles within. The girls' cheaply-blonde hair fell over their faces. They looked identical to one another, as if each drop of individuality had been sucked from them. The ends of their jeans were frayed. They would have names like Martina, Samantha and Jackie, she mused. Suddenly she rebuked herself for her unkindness. Life did not dole out advantages to everybody. She had been lucky. Well, a little more than merely lucky, but life had been good to her. Why, then, spend the better half of the morning despising those who were less well-off, who lived simpler lives?

The bus coughed loudly and stopped. The doors at the front opened. People prepared themselves, shuffled about as if no longer so eager to disembark. She sat watching them from the back of the bus. She would let everyone get off, then she'd leave. No sense in getting involved with a crush or an unnecessary queue.

Now she was in the street, feeling the pleasant weight of people around her, pressing at her from all sides. Voices, snippets of conversation overheard, laughter; the world surrounded her, washed over her. She walked through it all, happy, comforted. She went into shops, looked at very expensive dresses, even tried on one or two, feeling deliciously guilty under the watchful eye of security cameras and uniformed security men. She admired her figure in long mirrors. Years dripped away under the deceptive eye of imagination. Richard should be pleased with what he'd got, she thought. She passed buskers, dirty-looking young girls with rings in their nostrils and their hair plaited sitting cross-legged beside ragged young men who tried to play guitars and sang in rough, provocative tones. They seemed to dare the world to resent them. She walked around them, the girls smiling mischievously up at her, their hands out, palms upwards, begging for money, challenging her to walk by. She could feel their anger scorch her legs as she moved quickly past them. It had nothing to do with her. The welfare system over here was too damned soft anyway. Richard had often said that. Hadn't he? Yes, she'd heard him say that. Often.

The place had changed – town? city? – and she wondered where this shop had gone, what had become of that hairdressers. But she moved on, head down, sure of herself. By now she had accumulated a few odds and ends, a pleated skirt, a printed headscarf, a glossy magazine. She carried brightly coloured polythene bags. The sun ducked behind a bank of sinister dark clouds, but she kept her sunglasses on. She had lost track of time. There were more people in the street than ever. She looked up to see where she was. Not far from Richard's office, as it turned out. Would she 'phone him, surprise him, for lunch? Butterflies stirred in her belly. Perhaps if she called up to his office, perhaps if he closed and locked his office door . . .

A drunk staggered into the middle of the street causing a bus to stop hurriedly and drivers to honk their horns. He looked at her, looked away. He was singing, or trying to. Then he was cursing, swearing venomously at the bus, the town, the world. He made his way to the pavement and waved at nothing. The world passed him by. He was invisible in a strange sort of way. She shuddered. The people on the streets were passing her by too. She abandoned the idea of phoning Richard. She was cold, suddenly. The sun's heat was quenched for the moment. She looked for and found a well-known and very fashionable café. Dark wood panelling and waitresses dressed up like Victorian maids. A comforting, coffee-smelling place. Friendly lunchtime bustle. She went in, took off her glasses and looked around her as she stepped into a queue.

She chose a sticky bun – she felt incredibly daring, even a little bit naughty in a schoolgirlish fashion – and coffee without milk. Behind her the queue tailed out towards the front door. There was a great busy noise in the café. With considerable difficulty she found an unoccupied chair by the big front window. A gentle uncertain rain began to patter against the glass, little baby-fingers tapping shyly. Was there anything she should bring home for the children? Anything for Richard? He had given her so much. She was always grateful. She looked out into the busy lunchtime street, nibbled her sticky bun, sipped her strong black coffee. One worked hard to secure oneself in life. The rewards were infinite.

Someone had left a copy of the *Irish Times* on a chair. She reached over and picked it up. The court reports were dreadful abominations: rapes, assaults, embezzlements. The world was full to the brim with cruelty of all sorts. She couldn't read much of this and turned the pages noisily. Reports from India, Bosnia, Central America, Northern Ireland – violence, uncertainty, disruption. It was all too much. Surely newspaper editors could find something else to fill their pages. She read some film reviews and folded the newspaper over. She had time on her hands, now. She was restless. All around her were men and women looking busy over cups of tea, cream cakes, newspapers, and brightly clad children too young for school. She could feel the pulse of the city, like dark blood running under her feet. She looked down at the folded newspaper and a half-face of a weeping woman stared back at her. There were things that had to be ignored if one were to survive. At a far table, under a gaudy red sign indicating the smoking section, a group of teenagers with shaved heads and rings in their ears and nostrils laughed bitterly, savagely, and looked around them. She realised she was afraid of them. She stood up, annoyed that the legs of the chair made so much noise scraping on the floor. The waitresses in Victorian servant outfits moved from table to table tidying, cleaning up, serving meals. Everything in the café was raw brazen energy. She felt better out on the street.

Now some little bird of anxiety began to bite at her, pecking away as she moved off down the street. She wanted to bump into Richard and she was afraid to. She was appalled to realise that she didn't know what to do with herself. She scurried up the broad steps of a church. Inside, the silence struck her across the face. Old women moved around the Stations of the Cross with agonising patience. In front of which particular icon would the miracle begin? The ancient, familiar, comforting odour of stale breath and incense and wood polish clung to her like an old friend. The altar seemed very far away, white and gleaming. Above it, tall coloured windows filtered the sunlight into shards of reds, blues, yellows. She made her way into a pew, settled her various bags beside her, knelt down on the rubber step and closed her eyes and covered her face with her hands. She prayed. At first she recited prayers learned long ago. Our Father, Hail Mary, the Confiteor. As a child she had loved the mystery and ritual of the Latin Mass. There had been comfort in the unintelligible ceremony. One's faith was cleaner, more distinct, under the protective covering of Latin. She began to ask for things – one should never ask God for things, it wasn't right, really – but she asked for a secure life for her children and happiness for herself and Richard. She asked that she would pass her driving test. She began to feel rather silly, so she finalised everything by blessing herself, making the sign of the cross. She got out of the church, dipping two fingers in the cold water in the stone font at the big main door, dripping the holy water over her forehead. She wondered what the old women did with themselves when they had completed a round of the Stations. Did they simply start all over again? She shuddered at the bleakness of lives spent in churches, going round and round and round. There was, after all, an end to things. No doubt some of those women had once been young wives with families around them, had known joys and comforts, a lover's embrace. She shivered again. It was good to get back into the crowds; lose oneself. She turned a corner, not quite knowing where she was going, and there was Richard on the other side of the street, people shoving past him on either side. He was laughing and tapping a woman carelessly on the shoulder, and she was laughing too at whatever it was he was saying: well-dressed, young, eager-eyed, she was looking up into Richard's face.

It took a moment or two to see the other man, the one with his arm around the young woman's shoulder. Her heart slowed down; she realised she was standing stock-still in the middle of the pavement. Had she really thought that Richard and this young woman . . .? Of course not. But she had. Of course she had. She groped frantically for her sunglasses and put them on.

She watched Richard move away, wave at the couple, disappear into the crowd. She knew then why she was in town, why she was in more often in a week than was really necessary, why she didn't know what to do with herself. She stood there and let the cold unacknowledged dread creep over her, cover her from toe to head. Every morning he went off to work, she was terrified of losing him somehow, that he would never come back. That he was having an affair. She had always been afraid,

afraid of being on her own, of ending up like those old women in the church, of betrayal, of becoming just another face in the crowd. She detested herself for feeling such fear. In a way, it was a betrayal of them both. He had another life, a life that did not involve her, that took him away from her every morning. Nothing could make up for that, nothing ever *had*. Not the children, not the house, the location in the country, not their passionate love-making. She had done well to cover her true feelings, to dilute them with her own lies of routine.

She began walking, went into a lounge bar. Dreadfully sad music drifted down from the wall-speakers. The place was crowded, noisy. She found a vacant stool at the bar and ordered a drink. She had never done anything like this in her entire life. The drink came, a gin-and-tonic with ice. The young, grease-haired barman took her money and moved away without a glance at her. She sipped at the drink and caught sight of her face reflected in the mirror. Her terror began to dissolve. She removed her sunglasses.

Julie knew who she was now. A well-dressed woman sitting at a bar in the middle of the day drinking gin. Alone.

Daft

My son the nut.

Don't call him that, my father says. He's different. *You* were different. He bends forwards out of the wheelchair and grunts and tries to pick up a daffodil he's dropped out of a bunch he has on his lap. I move around, pick it up for him and put it back with the rest. I get behind the wheelchair again, where he can't see me or look into my eyes. Over his head and over the lines and lines of white flashing gravestones and then over the bright unharvested fields, the city of Belfast, where we were both born, where both of us grew up, hums like a wheel spinning; you can almost hear it. The Black Mountain so hot in the sun it has almost disappeared into a deep blue-black haze, the cranes of the shipyard yellow and arrogant, the streets crawling away this way and that, up Divis, out towards Holywood. The roar of an aircraft engine, the spit-and-rattle of a prowling helicopter – the sounds are constants, like something in a complicated algebraic problem. There is nothing you can do with them, nowhere to put them. My father looks down at his wife's grave, my mother's grave, says nothing, then mutters a prayer. All the time the daffodils sing in his lap and he does nothing about them. In the end he asks me to lay them out on the grave or put them in a jar if there *is* one. All the time the sun beats down like an open palm on the top of our heads and my mouth is dry and I long for a cold glass of lager. My father has grown more patient with age. And illness. He knows he is ill. For a long time he could fool himself that he was not, or that it wasn't so bad. But now, since the wheelchair, he has been unable to do so. Yet it doesn't seem to bother him.

Don't call him names, son, my father says. They'll stick. They'll grow with him. He'll start feeling inferior or something. Just as well no-one started calling *you* names or where would you be now?

Yes, where indeed? Off in the distance, tending other graves, are a group of young women in mourning black. The lines of graves here have grown longer, the headstones newer, in the past twenty years since my mother died. Violence has looked after all that. Bomb-victims, shooting-victims, stabbing-victims, all have found a place here, there being no sectarianism in death. I suspect some of the graves contain only parts of people. That's the way it goes. But the country air is sweet here, birds jabber away in the trees, the sky is admirably blue. If you listen carefully, you might hear cattle lowing somewhere in the distance. No armoured vehicles, no soldiers. Just people mourning and quietly remembering while the sun shines and birds sing. My father indicates something with an abrupt swing of his arm. His clothes barely fit him, he's lost so much weight. I have come, finally, to know who he is and was, and it breaks my heart to see this man in a wheelchair. I love him intolerably.

Clean that away, the scum or dead leaves or whatever it is there, look.

I clear away a whole pattern of dried-up leaves and dusty twigs. He leans forwards and back, as if he is balanced entirely on the base of his spine. Perhaps he is, for his legs are virtually paralysed and this will gradually worsen until hospital will be the only course of action. He knows all of this but won't ever talk about it. He knows also that this is where he will be buried, that I will have to look after things, and he *doesn't* know that *I* know that already he has spoken to his solicitors and cleared insurance policies and things like that out of the way. He was always like that, a man who detested trivia and humdrum difficulties. Get everything sorted out as soon as you can. Then you don't have to worry about it ever again. And never inconvenience anyone. I will never have qualities like that. Some parts of my life will always be a mess.

Anyway, when are you going over to see him, your wee Tommy? Why don't you bring him over one of these long evenings and you can drive us all out to Shaw's Bridge or maybe even Bangor? You're awful mean since you got that car.

My father acts as if I neglect my only child, my son. I too am an only child, I do not like any form of neglect or being left alone or out on the edge of things. So I am very considerate towards my son. I just don't like the politicking that I have to do around his mother, my wife. We are separated and it's just as well, we did not get on. She's doing well for herself these days and works in the telephone exchange. I, by the way, look after the shop. The shop my father and mother bought in the late 1940s shortly after they were married; the little corner shop on the street where they lived all those years, where I was born. Where the sun shines in a slant on one side of the street only and, in the back lanes, everybody learned to ride a pushbike and there were only outside toilets up to a few years ago and coal was dumped in heaps against a whitewashed back-yard wall and the next-door neighbours kept racing-pigeons.

When I was a kid the other kids in the street treated me with admirable ambiguity. In a game of street soccer, if I scored a goal, the other side would beat me up and call me nasty names to do with my religious persuasion; if I was a 'keeper and let one in, my own side would beat me up and go through the same ritual. My faults and virtues were the result of having the wrong religion. I got used to it. In the end, I could not even begin to imagine a street society in which discrimination and some sort of punishment were not a way of life. I loved my street-mates, I thought they were the best in the world. I would scrap at their side, rob orchards with them, even court their sisters in the dark alleys. But it was perfectly natural that they should, when the mood took them, turn against me and drag out the worn slogans and blasphemous songs. I took it to be part of their affection for me and it was years before I grew to detest it, to understand how innocent those kids had been compared with the weight of terror and madness and hatred lurking in the souls of their catch-phrases. But there I was, working in the shop, unable to do anything else or be anywhere else. All those kids were grown up and gone away. Every time there was a particularly nasty act of violence nearby, their old fathers and mothers would shuffle in slippers into the shop to commiserate with me. Salt of the earth. I loved them, loved the street I grew up in. Everything I had ever endured was part of it. Even the bits I hated, I hated with affection.

So it was that calling my son a nutcase was also a term of affection. He was fourteen and had begun to assert his individuality in school, a place of uniforms, Friday benedictions and clerics who roamed the polished corridors like great black birds of omen. During an English literature class he'd wanted to know why, in the past twenty years, no distinctly Loyalist poems or novels had emerged; in the middle of a history class, when a nasty anti-Protestant pogrom of the 1600s was being described and cheering broke out at the back of the room, my son the nut put up his hand and asked his teacher whether he shouldn't teach them to be ashamed of such episodes. Blows rained on his shoulders and the back of his head from less liberal-minded students. My son the nut. When I asked him about these incidents, he replied that he had no idea what drove him against the grain, but that it seemed the most natural and comfortable attitude to take. My son was incapable of blind hatred. My son the nut.

And get those glasses of his changed, says my father; the ones he has make him look like ET.

I'm beginning to sweat, gently, seductively. I stare over my father's balding head, and feel his feebleness and fragility course through the air like stained blood. The mourners at the far graves are wiping their eyes, lifting their black veils, looking around at the yards and yards of official death. It hasn't rained for days and the smell of earth is hot and dry. I think of my wife Belinda (yes, yes, I know). Tommy inherits his short-sightedness, his near-blindness, from Belinda the telephonist. Corn-dirty hair and big eyes always behind glass, like exotic fish in a tank. She kept them on even when making love. Her hair is shaved so close to her head in imitation of some pop star she's seen photographs of that she looks like a moulting owl. She has an accent that, my father said on first hearing it ten years ago, would chip glass. She came from an area of Belfast that was all wee streets of houses bordering the docks until bombs and development flattened it. My father adopted the old Belfast snobbishness and rarely spoke to her. She's not *refined*, was his verdict, as if my poor wife had been sugar. Or crude oil. And she was very, very small.

My son Tommy is lanky and will be my height when he grows up, if he survives long enough with his against-the-grain streak. His interests include football and making model aircraft – I always buy him a new kit when I take him out and then Belinda rings me up at the shop and tells me his room is cluttered with the things and why don't I teach him something useful and stop buying him model aircraft, the smell of glue and paint is giving her a headache, what do I think she lives in, Buckingham Palace with a load of rooms? Click. I think Belinda is seeing a man. I hope she is.

I have grown much closer to my father since my mother died. That was a long time ago and we've become more like big and little brother now. I do not know what I will do when he passes away (*dies* is a word we don't use much). There is something in him, a rugged Belfast thing, that I can depend on. He is the redbrick of the little money-box houses and the solid stone of the City Hall. The rust of the shipyard cranes is in his blood and the dust of the ropeworks is in his hair; his breath smells of the odour of baking bread which hangs in the air over the little streets of East Belfast near the big bakery; his moods are as quick to change as the colour of the water in the Lagan River. His voice can contain the roar of men on football terraces both sides of the city on Saturday afternoons when a goal is scored. And it can be as gentle as the murmurs of the old women in slippers and aprons, arms folded, standing outside their front doors gossiping. He has seen Orange parades pass by and admired their glamour and sound, while knowing what they symbolised and how untouchable they were. Until he went into the wheelchair, he went every month to Confession and approached the altar-rail for Communion with his head bowed like a schoolkid. If you could tap into his head, you'd see a whole history of Belfast. He's even grown small and wiry like Belfastmen do. All that is missing is the flat duncher cap.

When he goes, it is as if a whole part of something much greater will go with him. He saw the violence in York Street in the 1930s; he's reared his son up through the present row. In between was the World War and the nights Belfast got hit and St Anne's Cathedral was cut in half. And there he was, with lots more like him, scurrying back to life each time. And he fears for me, for my safety. He thinks I'll be alone and vulnerable when he's gone, alone in that corner shop. The one time we went on a holiday, taking Tommy, the violence came up and slapped us in the face. There was a bomb scare on the railway line coming back from Dublin; food in the restaurant ran out, booze ran out, the train crawled and crawled forever along the line while helicopters pranced up and down overhead. People played cards, children got tired and irritable, the rest of us were all afraid. We were allowed out of the carriages near Portadown. There was a British squaddie on the platform, there were squaddies all the length of the train. I asked this one what was going on, as if we didn't know, and he said I don't know mate and I don't bloody care. All I want is to get back to the wife and kids in Germany in a fortnight, not get blown up by a Paddy bomb. And I said fair enough and got back on the train. My son Tommy went into hysterics and screamed I want to get off I want to get off and we had to restrain him, hold him down between us while he went into fits of tears all the way back to Belfast and I know he suffers from claustrophobia now and always will, in small rooms or in crowds.

My father fears for me because he thinks sometimes I'm still Tommy's age, and sometimes he's right. He tells me things are changing, that, in a few years, the signs are, things will change *completely*. Belfast is a lively, witty, busy wee place and always was, my father tells me, on evenings when I bring him a copy of the *Telegraph* and he sits in the wheelchair reading it, taking inspiration of an almost religious nature from its pages. The people of Belfast are *resilient*, he says, even though no article in the paper may have started off this train of thought; they bounce back always like rubber balls. Best in the world, son. Been through it all before, don't forget. Came back. Built the *Titanic*. The city gets bigger every day and, son, you can't beat the Belfast sense of humour.

Sometimes he displays this sense of humour by telling Tommy, lifting up the boy's thin arms, that there's more meat on a crutch.

Up in the air – it's hard to look up, but up there somewhere – a rogue helicopter is venturing out of the city and over the hills and the peaceful countryside, chattering, muttering, like an old man on wings. Immediately you feel looked at, spied upon, guilty. You don't feel like looking up, in case someone takes your photograph. My father raises his head, the mourners raise theirs. What about ye? My father yells, waving his two hands in the air. *See* enough?

Embarrassed, no doubt, by my father's waving and shouting, the thing turns in a circle and heads back over the city. My father has always believed that the ordinary man, what he terms the ordinary 'five-eighths', could always influence things if he tried.

A union man in his single days, some old boys still remembered him. Jimmy, they say; aye, he was a right wee terrier. Before he met my mother – in the black-out, in the war – he worked in a bakery and there are photographs of him, with moustached men either side, aprons on, arms folded. He looks dangerously handsome, dark-eyed, hair parted right down the middle of his head: a back-street Valentino waiting to be discovered. I've heard those old men who knew him back then say he could have been anything he wanted, but what he wanted was the bakery and then my mother and then the shop, pitching his tent in the middle of Belfast, tying up the old camel for good.

Silence folds over the cemetery once again and with it comes a light and welcome breeze. The mourners start to pick things up, move away, feel embarrassed. My father watches them and then, suddenly, I feel his fingers on the fingers of my left hand. He says nothing, then their weight slips away as if he too had become embarrassed about something. Did you say a prayer for your Ma, son? he asks me. Yes, Da, I lie. Then take me away out of this.

I pull the wheelchair back from the edge of the grave, ease back my weight on the wheels, raise the front, turn it away. My father is always silent during these manoeuvres; he detests his helplessness. The sun is hot on the tarmac pathways, the wide curving road from the gate. The mourners at the other graves are moving away with a grateful dignity, free again. The dead linger in the blood here. My father clears his throat. What time is it? he asks me. He's forgotten his wristwatch again, the one I gave him for his last birthday with his name inscribed on the back. I tell him what time it is. He seems to be ladling time out into the soup-bowl of his life with careful, delicately measured draughts. He is afraid, yet he has accepted his fear as he accepts his illness. He is stronger than I imagine I would ever be in similar circumstances.

Another hour till my medication, my father pronounces as we trundle downhill, my heels digging into the tarmac, braking us. Another hour and then them wee white pills.

It's the red ones in the afternoon, I correct him. I am his nurse now, the simpler role of son has been usurped. I am more important than a son; without me he would not be able to live. Aye, the red ones, if you say so. You're good at remembering things. I'm hopeless, says my father.

I feel his weight in the wheelchair, a child's weight, the weight I was, or close to it, when we took the obligatory Sunday drives in his battered Standard Eight down to Helen's Bay, Millisle, or Bangor. The Helen's Bay trip meant paddling your feet in the waters of Belfast Lough and now and then sighting a slow-moving ship; Millisle was the big white windmill, silent and always shut because it was Sunday, and Bangor was putting pennies into the big re-painted mine for the Lifeboat Institute. Then there were wee fat men sandwiched between billboards crying at the bathers to repent, repent, the end was nigh. Big faces of boarding-houses overlooking the promenade like tired old Victorian matrons. Shy-eyed wee girls in one-piece bathing suits. Ice-cream melting down my fingers. Bangor Rock, with the word 'Bangor' stamped right through to the last crunch. Always, the primal salty odour of the sea and the hot light-headedness of having so many people around. My mother dressed in flowing coloured headscarves and my father donned sunglasses and sleeveless shirts. Everyone was friendly on the promenade, no religion, no factions, nothing.

Days so holy that when I think of them I am filled with the same sense of awe that I once felt as a child listening to the words in Latin, the tinkling of altar bells, my head bowed, terrified to look up; a mystery, profound, beatific, unique. My father would nudge me, push me out in front of him. The two of us, followed by my mother, would approach the immaculate linen draped over the marble rail; in those moments nothing was more important than what we were engaged in, time stopped, a new order of things was created. When I recall my Sunday afternoon outings, my memories are immaculate and sacred. Breakfast would be waiting back home; my stomach would ache with hunger. The day would stretch away into an infinity of possibilities; the closed curtains of the rest of the empty street did not deter me. The sun would creak on the cobblestones and on the pavement and not a child stirred any-where. Forbidden to go out and enjoy themselves, they would disappear. As we drove out of the city, we passed playgrounds with their swings tied up and their gates locked.

By the sea, it seemed, life was different.

My father grunts slightly, pain has started in on him again. Down by the open-mouthed gateway the other mourners are climbing into cars and someone's cracking jokes to relieve the tension of grief. Whoever he was, my father said, he probably didn't make them laugh so much when he was alive.

My modest chariot gleams silver and blue in the sunlight, waiting with a patient look on its face. My father stares at my car. Change your oil regularly? I thought it felt a wee bit slug-gish on the way up. Yes, Da, I say. I change it like clockwork. Points alright? Yes, Da. You want to keep an eye on the engine, son, I think you overdo the gear changes a bit. That car's near-ly ten years old, for God's sake. Yes, Da, but it's got a brilliant engine and I *do* take care of it. You'd want to, he says; you'd not want the bother of getting a new car with the price of them now. Do you remember the wee Standard I used to have? I was just thinking about it, Da. Wee wheeker, that wee bus.

I open the door, slide him out of the wheelchair like slipping a pea out of a pod, wait until he's settled and collapse the chair. We are so close now, so united by one thing and another. We drive over a ridge and the city of Belfast is lying beneath us like a coloured blanket. There are so many things I want to know from him, to learn, and I am terrified he will be gone before I can begin. He stares out through the windscreen and I know he is picking out landmarks. There's the mill your granny worked in, there, look. I can't take my eyes off the road, Da, I tell him. There's the public baths I taught you to swim in, look. I can't. Och, it's gone now. The city is lovely in the sun, my father says.

Yes, it is very lovely in the sun, all its buildings clear and sharp-focused, the green dome of the City Hall leaping out from everything. I drive, thinking of how much we will never say, how big the hole in my heart will be. You said I was different, Da, I ask him: what did you mean I was different?

He keeps staring through the windscreen at the city, at the streets, the buildings, and his eyes are wet and I know he doesn't want me to look at him.

Och, you were just different, son, my father says. Always a wee bit daft.

The Hammer Man

What my Uncle Tommy did was, he got very angry and hit my Aunt Anna with a hammer until she was dead and then he carried her upstairs to the big bed in the front room overlooking their garden and he wrapped her up in a sheet and other bedclothes and left her there for a couple of weeks.

My Uncle Tommy was a small, round man, always laughing, always making jokes about his billiard-ball head, always the funny man at family parties. He and Aunt Anna had no kids, so they loved everyone else's and made a big deal about me because I sang songs and was called *talented* by my mother, Uncle Tommy's sister. I would get a pat on the head, money, bars of chocolate. This was a long time ago and kids still appreciated these things. At any rate, Uncle Tommy kept coming over to our house, even with his wife tucked up dead in bed, and it was at our house that he was arrested.

I put most of this together later, but I can still remember the clean, serious, hard faces of the detectives in their plain suits as they came in, blundered in, through the kitchen. They probably reckoned Uncle Tommy would try to make a run for it out the back door. But if they'd thought to ask me I would have told them Uncle Tommy wasn't like that. He had *spirit*. The only reason he left Aunt Anna in the bed was because he was trying to arrive at a strategy by which he might deal with what had happened. Not because, as they said in court, he was a coward.

The police came in and wouldn't accept a chair or a cup of tea, and my father, who disliked Uncle Tommy immensely, tried to calm my mother down and Uncle Tommy sat in the front room, where a moment before he'd been telling me a funny story, staring at his hands and humming something to himself. Before they took him away, I saw that he was crying quietly, trying not to let anyone see. As if it was all too much to make public. But it got public soon enough.

Every newspaper had a photograph, a bad one, of Uncle Tommy and Aunt Anna. I must tell you here that Aunt Anna was Greek. She had very dark hair, eyes black and deep as holes, a big round smiling face and a loud voice with which she tried out her bad English. They'd met in a dance hall in the days when dance halls were the big thing and everyone met there. There is a wedding photo: Uncle Tommy smiling, wearing too-wide trousers and a double-breasted suit, my mother carrying flowers and looking flirty, my father serious and looking at Aunt Anna who, of course, was dressed in vicious white. She was a war orphan; her entire family had been shot somewhere in the Greek mountains and she did not ever want to go back. Now and then this big jovial woman would drink too much and break down and mutter away to herself on the sofa in Greek; names and places, I suppose. I was a kid. But I recognised defeat when I saw it.

In Dublin, she worked as a waitress, learned just enough English to get a sort of promotion, took a few casual lovers, met Uncle Tommy and got married. The whisper was that she couldn't have any kids of her own because there was something inside her gone twisted or wrong because of what had happened back in the war in Greece. Aunt Anna, it seemed, had been with some teenage boyfriend when her house had been raided by the Germans and her family were taken off. Whatever she and her boyfriend had been doing, it was said discreetly that she had taken a kitchen knife to her stomach and stabbed herself repeatedly with it on hearing of the destruction of her family. Aunt Anna drank a lot; so, in the end, did Uncle Tommy. They'd seldom turn up at our house sober.

Dublin, at the time when Uncle Tommy and Aunt Anna had their most serious and final disagreement, was a comfortable village sort of place. People went about without any fear of being mugged or attacked or robbed. Everyone seemed to know everyone else. You could walk, as a kid, up O'Connell Street and your mother would be saying big hellos right and left like an actress and there were always men stopping to talk to your father. The buses were green and you could swing off the silver bar at the entrance at the back where you got on. Grafton Street had the coffee smells of Bewley's Oriental Café, hard sunlight or soft, sad rain, kids shouting out the evening editions of the papers, the sharp lazy sound of horses' hooves on the street where Arthur Guinness and others still used to transport wooden casks of stout and beer about on wagons that rolled on iron-rimmed wheels. Nelson was still up there on his monument near the Gresham Hotel, single-eyeing the whole city, down towards the Liffey, up to the mountains and the craggy ruin of the Hellfire Club. It was a friendly, philosophical city. It was emerging from darker times when people lived ten to a room in tenements and whole families died from tuberculosis. Sure, not everyone had money. But money went further then, or seemed to. The city of Dublin was a good place to grow up in, or at least I thought so. And Uncle Tommy had to go and spoil it all by hammering Aunt Anna.

Newspapers had their photos, the radio had reports. Virtually no one had a TV, so we were spared that. I saw Uncle Tommy's smiling face on newspaper stands; I watched Aunt Anna watching me in shops where they sold magazines and papers and displayed a special poster advertising the trial reports. People, all sorts of people, especially our neighbours, muttered as they walked past our house. Then they stopped walking past. Then they started not to sit beside us at Mass on Sundays. Then one Sunday the priest delivered a sermon on Cain hammering Abel and my mother grabbed me by the hand, ignoring the embarrassed protests of my father, and dragged me out of the Roman Catholic Church forever.

There was a weedy, green-watered canal running down the back of our house and, creeping away just to be on my own, I'd go there. Old winos hung about there, but they slept or scrounged during the day and I was safe enough. Now and then the bloated carcass of a dog would drift by and I'd wonder, or begin to wonder, what Aunt Anna's face had looked like after a couple of weeks wrapped up dead in bed. That was when I forced myself to read the newspaper accounts of the trial, read them in secret where possible, huddling up in the outside toilet to read the pages I'd stuffed up my jersey.

What those reporters brought out about Aunt Anna and Uncle Tommy was unbelievable, scandalous. I thought they were writing about two other people, certainly not the people I'd known – and, let's face it, loved. Uncle Tommy drank, I knew, and Aunt Anna drank too; but these fights, voices raised in the night, complaints from neighbours, the police being called over and over – I knew nothing of this. Aunt Anna's screams, it was said, could be heard all the way down their street on many occasions, with the sounds of things being knocked about and broken. A hell-house, for sure. Neighbour after obliging neighbour took the stand and described times when Aunt Anna had been seen to skulk in the front garden to read a paper, wearing dark glasses even though the sun wasn't shining. Others recalled seeing Uncle Tommy weeping as he walked down the street. Many times. It went on and on as if it were never meant to end. Uncle Tommy did not deny what he'd done. His defence endeavoured to prove that he hadn't been in his right mind when he'd done what he'd done. But the prosecution case rested comfortably on the notion that, since

the hammer that had silenced Aunt Anna for good had always
been kept in a locked toolbox in the basement, Uncle Tommy
had given a degree of calculated thought to going down to get
it, bring it upstairs and kill Aunt Anna. Now that I've typed the
word I see how horrible a little word it is, so laden with meaning; that's, after all, what Uncle Tommy had done. He'd *killed*
her. Then, of course, there was the business of wrapping her
up in bedclothes and leaving her on the bed. Premeditation.
He'd thought it all out, they said. But then, said the defence,
there was the *other man*.

At first there were allegations, things neighbours said, and
it's lucky for some of them you can't libel the dead. No one ever
remembered seeing a face, hearing a late night taxi draw up, or
hearing rhythmic noises through the walls, nothing like that.
But he began to grow out of rumour and quickly turned into a
concept and then to an absolute certainty in three or four trial
days. Aunt Anna had been seeing someone on the side. Several people. Uncle Tommy knew and must have been driven to
distraction. Uncle Tommy's defence people were happy enough
with themselves.

About the time this stuff started to appear in the papers, my
father stopped attending the trial. My parents had been done
with as witnesses fairly early on, but my mother still went every
day and my father went with her. Now he stopped, he stayed at
home. He lurched about from one room to another, not saying
much, trying his best to act reasonable with me. He tended to
what we had of a garden, listened to various unrelated things on
the radio, made countless cups of tea. Some days he wouldn't
bother to shave. There were long silences between himself and
my mother, things you could almost reach out and touch. There
were intense periods when, the three of us sitting in the one
room, the silence threatened to drown us like a wave. In these
periods I was most afraid. I did not know what of, but the fear
was real and heavy. I began to go off my food. My mother took
me to see our doctor. He examined me all over and asked me if
I had a cough or pain in my chest. No. Well, like everybody else

in the world, he knew about Uncle Tommy and Anna. He told my mother I appeared to be depressed, though I was young for it. Kids were not supposed to get depressed in those days, it was a grown-up's illness. At any rate, he prescribed a pick-me-up and some sleeping pills. I was a kid, on sleepers. When I *think* of it. Thank you again, Uncle Tommy.

The trial continued, the reports kept appearing in the papers, the neighbours slipped past our door blessing themselves. Every detail, every private moment of the life lived out between my Uncle Tommy and Aunt Anna became public property. Gradually it all got to be slightly unreal, a story in the papers, things happening to other people, nothing to do with me, my parents. Then I started getting it in the neck at school.

At first it was sniggers behind hands, back-of-the-classroom mutterings. Then I began to understand that my teachers themselves read newspapers, listened to radios, concocted a variety of gossip peculiarly their own. Some of them regarded me – in the hallways, classrooms, in the yard – with curiosity, watching me, saying nothing, waiting for me to do something strange and in keeping with being the nephew of a murderer. And of a *murderee*, of course. I found myself holding myself in, almost a physical sensation. I would hug myself tightly, my arms wound around my chest and my fingers almost touching across my back. I was some talked-about species of strange animal, watched and observed at all times, my behaviour monitored. Others cleared their throats as they entered the room, as they walked passed me in corridors. I embarrassed them. They had not come across my like before. They had no way of dealing with me. The usual ridiculous offerings of trite condolences, the kind of thing you got if a relative or parent died, didn't work here. Then the other kids started.

Watch him, he's the hammer-man! Look out, here comes hammer-head! Hey! Where did you hide your granny (mother, father, aunt, anyone) – up in the bed? Look out, you can smell his dead aunt off him! Lying up in the bed with the worms eating her! Hey, hammer-head!

Thank you yet again, Uncle Tommy.

Once, maybe twice, I fought back. Then I grew tired of it.
You couldn't keep your guard up, be in a state of alert and
readiness all the time. It wore you out. The taunting stopped,
or at least it went underground. Just as the neighbours passed
our front door as if we were lepers, now the kids avoided my
desk, refused to sit with me, made me take my lunch alone.
One particular lunchtime I thought I had a companion, but he
just wanted to know if I'd been up in the bedroom and seen the
bed my aunt had been in all the time she was dead. When I
said I hadn't, he shrugged his shoulders and moved off.

Now and then my mother visited Uncle Tommy. You could
always tell when she'd been to see him. She would barge into
the house, saying nothing, bustling through to the kitchen,
messing about with the kettle, dishes, making a lot of unnecessary noise. Often she'd call me into the kitchen and give me
a list of messages and send me out to the shops for an hour. It
wouldn't take an hour, but I'd go down by the canal, laze about,
reluctant to go back home, to the silences, all of it. Besides, I
had the feeling that no one would miss me. I was most of the
time in a state of drowsiness, on account of the sleeping pills
the doctor had prescribed taking their time wearing off during
the day. In school I'd often enough trip over desks. Of course,
I was ignored. So I'd go out for these errands and take my time
down by the canal, hoping to meet a dead dog I could talk to.
Then there were the odd times when she'd call me into the
kitchen so that I could watch her crying. She seemed to need a
witness. She wasn't going to go through all this misery without
a witness. My father, meanwhile, sat in the front room cloaked
in silence and he seemed to shrink with each passing day. I told
myself, afraid of the notion, that one day I'd look for him in the
front room and hear a tiny squeak come from the armchair and
there he'd be, my father, half an inch tall.

The revelations that my Aunt Anna – she had been buried
with only my parents and myself, drenched in a downpour, to
mourn her – had been, as I heard a teacher describe it, *passing*

it around, caused strange fires to be lighted under my parents. Dark fires. Fires that burned slowly and had a lot of patience. My father's despair thickened like smoke. My mother tried to see her way through the smoke. Occasionally, she was nice to him, nice without saying a word. She brought him the papers. From their room at night, urgent noises came. Voices were raised. My mother's remained soft, gentle for a time, then lifted. My father's went straight up, straining for some note high in the air and beyond his reach. Then my mother would laugh. At the same time, I'd hear my father grunt as if he was lifting heavy weights. Then more of my mother's laughter. Then the sound of my father's fist hitting the bed-head. Then utter, dark, terrifying silence.

I understood that my mother was trying to work through the smoke so that she could taunt him about something. I didn't know what, then. I know now. My father retreated, grew angry, retreated some more. She came on, unstoppable. Always when she handed the newspaper to him – I noticed, with horror – it was open at an account of the trial. Then the nice touch, she'd bring him a packet of cigarettes. He wouldn't know what to say, to thank her or fling them in her face. I could tell. He'd open the packet as if it were wired to a bomb. My mother would cross her legs and let her skirt ride up embarrassingly about six inches above her knee. He'd try not to look at her legs; he'd light a cigarette, hands shaking.

A *slut*, I heard my mother say to him one day when she thought I wasn't there. A *whore*, that woman! My mother seldom used any sort of foul language. *There!* Read all about it. Half the town up on top of her. *Read it!*

I made myself scarce, let them get on with it. I felt more alone than at any time in my life, before or since.

The trial came to an end. The world seemed to heave a sigh of relief. Or was it regret? My Uncle Tommy – the clown, the jokester, the hammer man – got life, or thereabouts, all pleas of diminished this and that having been weighed and considered like so many bids at an auction. It seemed to me that the entire city of Dublin sympathised with him at the end. The trial over, and all succulent revelations dried up, our neighbours started talking over the gate to us again. My mother they started talking to on the very same day the verdict was handed down. The neighbours exchanged soothing sorrows, defeats, illnesses, which was their way of identifying with our pain. She wasn't, they pointed out, *one of us*. Meaning my Aunt Anna, that she was Greek and all that. She was different. Foreign, had *different ways*. Which might have meant she knew how to enjoy herself, for the neighbours could not contain their envy, their need of her. Hot blood, the neighbours said, tightening their grip on their wicker shopping bags, tying and re-tying their transparent plastic rain hoods. What that poor man must have suffered! Try the patience of a saint, foreign women. Stick to your own, they said. But you can always go up and visit him, they'd conclude by way of consolation. Just up the canal. Visiting days.

My father slipped away into the shadows of himself and didn't come out again. He started drinking, and going out to work no longer meant much to him. My parents began to fight. It was rougher now. You were damned lucky, my mother taunted him; *damned* lucky. Your name would have been *mud*. All our names!

My mother finally lost all interest in my father when President John F. Kennedy was shot in Dallas. She wept for days; the neighbours met her weeping at the gate and wept with her, pure Old Testament stuff. Such a nice Catholic boy, they said. A beautiful smile. And his poor wife. Did you see them when they were over here? God, he was *gorgeous*!

My mother bought a picture of the dead president and hung it up over the fireplace facing a similar picture of the Pope. In every chip shop in Dublin, the same two pictures grimaced at one another over the deep-fat fryers. In every little corner shop, Kennedy and the Pope waved at each other over the cigarettes and bars of cheap chocolate. The newspapers carried photographs, news, biographies, pictures of the Kennedy kids and of Jackie. Then of Lee Harvey Oswald. What was my Uncle

Tommy compared with him? But this time no one remembered much about Uncle Tommy and no one cared.

I was hardly surprised to come home from school one day, to find my mother crying in the kitchen – crying was nothing strange for her – and my father gone. Gone for good. He'd left a note. Of sorts, nothing fancy. Brief, to the point. He never loved me, my mother declared. He never loved you, either of us. Sniffle-sniffle. Over the stone sink and the metal clatter of pots and cutlery. Her hands plunged greedily into the sudsy water. The sun shone through the kitchen window and brightened her dull blonde hair. Once a fortnight she went to the hairdresser's on the corner and exchanged malicious gossip under the hairdriers. She needed to go there soon. I saw how lined and pale her face had become, a beautiful face, once. Her very blue eyes were wide and wet. I wanted to stroke her hair, kiss her face, dry the tears. But I just stood there listening, looking, not her kid anymore but a stranger visiting, passing through, noticing her, anxious to stop her crying. Embarrassed in my helplessness, I got out of there, headed for the comfort of the canal.

I didn't miss my father. He'd been going slowly for a long time. It was as if he'd just finally closed the door behind him. There was nothing to say, do, nothing. At school, rumours flew about but I ignored them. Hey! Hammer-head! That sort of thing. But it was played out now. It didn't last. Neighbours actually came right in to our house these days. My mother barricaded herself behind a brace of gaggling women and sipped whiskeyed tea. The neighbours seemed to be more welcome there than I was. They gave my mother something, and I reminded her of something and there you had the difference. At night, of course, she cried. You could hear it even with your bedroom door closed.

My father never came back. One day my Uncle Tommy did. Leaner, stooping, a hundred years older, all the joking gone out of him. He just appeared one day at the door. Whole lifetimes were written across his eyes. He lived in a tiny room in a boarding house, resisted my mother's immediate offers to stay with us, and now and then looked for work. But he was close to being an old man and the work thing was just to give himself something to do. He ended up spending a lot of time with his feet up in our house staring at the patterns on the wallpaper, saying nothing. There was no light of any kind in his eyes. He never said a word about what it was like to be in prison. Now and then I'd drive him around the altered city in my second-hand car and point out places that had changed or disappeared and then I realised this only made him feel worse. He'd nod, but never say anything. One day when he was at our house I came in and told him I was engaged to be married; told him before I told my mother. He nodded then too, wordlessly.

Of Aunt Anna he did not speak either. Never. Not a single word. And he did not ask one single question about my father, where he might have gone, if he wrote, nothing. For a while after he turned up, Uncle Tommy was a sort of dark celebrity in our street. Neighbours would say hello to him, smile at him, but he would barely raise his head. He had become a sort of hero to them, but he was too badly wounded to take heed. My mother made a point of burning all the newspapers she'd kept since the trial. As if, with Tommy out now, none of it had ever happened. My mother and Uncle Tommy were both dead before I discovered the love letters Aunt Anna had written to my father.

I was clearing out the old house, tired to death of the place, anxious to be gone. A heart attack had claimed Uncle Tommy alone, sleeping in his single rented room. He'd been dead a couple of days and was starting to go off a bit before the landlady bothered to have his door broken down; all of which had a certain weight of irony. My mother, crippled with early arthritis and her hair almost completely grey, took longer to die. Almost three years. Through all of it I tended to her, at home, later in the hospice, causing my wife to turn on me – what did your mother ever do for you, that sort of thing – feeling neglected, maybe even jealous. My mother died, drugged out of her mind, and I breathed more easily. My father did not turn up for the funeral. Perhaps he was dead by then too.

There they were, a carefully-tied-up bundle of old letters. In my mother's tidy bedside drawer. Had she taken them out at night, every night, all those years, and read them over and over? Well, I read them.

I read passion, honesty, heartbreak, longing, all that shared hot blood. I read love and anger, laughter, fear. My father had known that Aunt Anna was playing around with more than him and had told her so. She had tried to reassure him, played with him. Love talk. Baby talk. Bed talk.

The kind of stuff I'd heard in my own ear as I got older and stupider. The kind of stuff any man loves to hear. The words that, in the right order, conjure a magic that soothes him and lifts the world from his heart. My moon-faced Aunt Anna, the Greek war orphan. My runaway father. For how long? It read like years – I recalled my father's glance at her in that wedding photo, so how many years was *that*. She had, for her part, loved Uncle Tommy neither more nor less than she loved her other men. Being married to him didn't really count. She'd already lost all that she would ever love with any seriousness in this world; they had died in the same hour she'd been under her teenage boyfriend, the same hour she stabbed herself with grief and remorse and wished also to be dead. In one letter she'd gone so far as to explain all this to my father. *In bed yes I love you. In my heart there is only death.* Had Uncle Tommy found my father's letters back to her? Was that what had driven him finally into going for his hammer?

I kept those letters for a time, then burned them. They are of no interest to anyone. My father had taken his guilt and sorrow up on his back and gone off into the world with it, a penitent pilgrim of sorts. I trust – I really do – that he eventually found some sort of comfort somewhere.

For my part, I don't consider myself a jealous man, but the sight of a hammer in my house makes my stomach turn over. And this city has changed, has it ever. Murder is still news, but not front page news, and it has lost its uniqueness in a city of daylight muggers and coke-heads. Uncle Tommy wouldn't recognise the place. He wouldn't feel safe here. The rest of the modern world has visited what was once our little village and the prudent stay off the streets late at night. You don't leave the front door open for the neighbours to come in anymore.

We don't have any kids of our own as yet, but we're trying. Time enough. Most of the time we're happy. As happy as anyone else. But any time my wife and I have an argument she says, when I make her angry, that's my Uncle Tommy coming out in me. That makes me really mad. And sad, too.

Mad and sad. Just like he was, I suppose, that night all those years ago. Mostly sad.

Keeping the Night Watch

It grew dark. Everyone was hungry, cold. Here and there cigarettes flared up. Men breathed hard into their hands. A train clacked and banged over the railway bridge a hundred yards down the inlet and somewhere up in the air. Everyone was tired. They'd reached that point in a search where for ten minutes or an hour or a whole day there seems to be nothing left to do. A sort of embarrassment crept over everyone. They stood in the reeds in thigh-high floppy rubber leggings or sat in the jogging, leaky rowing boats with their legs wide apart and their knees at an angle into the air like patient fishermen; yet they had nothing to do, no new ideas, and they were cold and tired and needed a break and something to eat and it was darkening, darkening all around them. Besides, they looked to Quigley to make decisions and he couldn't make any.

Quigley couldn't do anything, hadn't the will, was miles away. He longed for some sort of space to open up through which he might disappear back into the city and put things right again with his wife, say it was not so bad that she was seeing another man, say that somehow they could work something out for the sake of the kids if for no other reason, and all the rest of it. Instead, he found himself in charge of a civilian search of the inlet, the banks, the reeds, the bend where the inlet became a river and where city sewers emptied their wasteload of shit, condoms, sanitary towels and anything else the city didn't want. He was looking for the body of a young man who'd been seen half a dozen nights before throwing himself into the river from the railway bridge. He couldn't care less at this stage. He'd been searching for two nights, two days. The police searched too, all those official uniforms working silently, never paying him or his volunteers the slightest notice. A sort of contempt for amateurs, he'd decided. But then he came to realise and acknowledge that the professionals were just as tired, bored and hungry as the rest of them. No amount of talking could relieve it. And all the time no one really wanted to find the body, because everyone could guess the condition it would be in after nearly a week in the water. Rats, too.

So now, the police gone for a time searching somewhere else, the horror-movie amphibians with their aqualungs and flippers and masks gone with them, Quigley and his crew sat and stood about idly and wanted to go home or to the nearest pub. After a little while, the old war stories started. If Quigley wouldn't tell them they could go and get something to eat, drink, or whatever, they'd smoke and tell old stories. The headless corpse so eaten away it was nearly all bone, the kitchen knife stuck between the ribs; the fat green bloated body bobbing up and down in the reeds like an enormous child's toy, the eyes gone. Stories like that. Everyone had one. The city had its share of people throwing themselves from the railway bridge. Sooner or later, men waded in and out the inlet and the river of their own volition, determined, then less so, to find the body. The body, everyone knew, could have drifted or been tide-towed just about anywhere. But the search, the volunteering, was a sort of ritual, a kind of cleansing that approached its own weight of spirituality. After a search, a volunteer felt different. It was hard to explain. Whether a body was found or not, it didn't seem to matter. You were different. If it was your first search, it was as if you belonged ever after to an elite, a sort of envied priesthood. And Quigley, a taxi driver by trade, was head man, top dog, the one who always walked into the police station when he'd read about someone seen going off the bridge, or when someone had brought him the news, and let it be known that his team were available to assist, and so on. He thought about them as his team, but really most of them would have gone down to the station in any case, Quigley or no Quigley, and offered to search with the police. It usually happened that Quigley was there, always had been, taking some sort of charge. He was a big man, fifties, a lot of thick black hair on his head, and he had a big voice. A son of the city, like the rest of them. So somehow he'd become their spokesman, and no one ever thought to object. They became his team.

But no on had seen him like this before. So indecisive, hesitant, lost. Now and then someone would risk a glance in his direction. No one was afraid of him. His awkwardness, his nervousness, made them feel embarrassed. A little ashamed, too. It was dark by now, and a couple of swans rose up like dirty blankets in the gathering breeze and thwock-thwocked their way into the night. Some of the men looked at them, saw the graceful noisy shapes banter through the low sky, and were grateful for something to look at. The two dogs in the bottom of one of the boats yapped lazily, then were silent again. The sounds carried out over the inlet. The lights of the city were all around, winking, glinting, coming on, traffic headlights moving like frightened things here and there, anxious little dots of white and red light. Quigley lit himself a cigarette, shielding the match from the breeze. He wanted to go back, find an excuse to go back. He pulled on his cigarette and, not taking it out of his mouth, told them they'd move up the inlet again towards the river, one last time, that was it. Then they'd call things off, enough for one day. No one looked at him.

They moved off through the reeds, their feet tugging at river weeds and clumps of watergrass, wading awkwardly, sucked down, the beams of half a dozen powerful torches slicing and angling through the heavy darkness. The boats made soft gliding sounds over the water. Quigley wanted to make up some excuse, get them all absorbed in what they were doing and break away, come back later. They'd be searching for an hour at least, he'd be home and say what he had to say and back out here and no one would even bother to ask him where he'd been. No one would miss him.

He stood for a while on the bank and watched the others darken and become black shapes doing a sort of slow weighted ballet through the water and reeds of the inlet. He heard the sigh of traffic on distant roads, the disturbed crack of waterbirds here and there, someone's abrupt laugh. He shouted that he'd be back in a short while, nothing more than that, and someone he could not recognise turned and waved in acknowledgement, then moved off with the others. Quigley felt diminished. Dismissed. Silly, of course, he told himself. They needed him. He pulled them together, gave them purpose, led them. If this wasn't true, then what was? They knew him, his dependability. They respected him. It took a good deal of thinking like this to reassure Quigley as he stood longer than he cared to on the edge of the inlet and looked after the rest of them as they dissolved into the wet darkness. He turned himself around and crouched, stumbled, felt his way up the bank to the road.

Once in his car he felt comforted, safe. The door slammed shut and the sounds of the night fell away. The interior of Quigley's car was thick with the suffocating odour of stale cigarette tobacco and male sweat. She had her own car; it was just as well. Coke tins rattled around on the floor as he pulled away from the kerb. Old newspapers, faded from sunlight through the rear window, shifted and crackled as the car leaned over to take a bend in the road. One day he'd clean it out. One day he'd get the passenger door fixed so that you didn't have to climb in over the driver's seat. Little things, but they mounted up, became big things. He was in slow traffic now, men going home from late office shifts, overtime, women heading out for the evening in twos and threes, a young buck with his windows down and a stereo blasting all over the road, thumpa-thumpa-thump. Quigley felt very tired. He closed his eyes for a moment, let the car roll on. He opened his eyes and slammed on the brake, a foot from a rear bumper. He hadn't the faintest idea what he was going to say to her. There was no quick way to repair something that had taken years to break. She'd told him straight to his face. Yes, she had *found love* somewhere else. *Found love*. The phrase had knifed him in the heart. Not a casual screw, no, it had to be love. The words drew his open palm after them and he struck her in the face. Not hard, just a frustrated, loose blow. She didn't even bother to put a hand to her cheek. She stepped back, looked at him, and laughed, shook her head. Predictable reaction, she said. No understanding why a woman does a thing like that, she said. A woman does things like that, goes out searching for love, companionship it starts out as probably but it ends up as love, and the man never understands why.

He'd stood in the middle of their living-room, she'd moved around him as if he were a rock in a river. He'd poured himself a stiff drink and followed her into the kitchen. I'm sorry, he said. And found he had nothing more to say; nothing to follow his apology with, nothing at all. Stupidly standing there, watching her fumble at something in the sink, he sipped his neat whiskey. There's nothing to say, she said, into the sink. He wasn't worth turning around and facing; he felt that, he felt she had all the good ways to hurt someone, to hurt him. After twelve years of marriage, you knew all the good ways.

Feeling silly, he'd turned and gone back into the living-room. She made him feel like a child, she was so good at that. Quigley drank, poured another, started looking frantically for his anger. He could hear her doing whatever she was doing to ignore him in the kitchen; upstairs, their youngest, their daughter Melanie – Quigley remembered his limp protestations at the name, how plastic it sounded, how damnably out of place, a name from a TV soap, not a proper name for a daughter of his, but his wife had brushed his arguments aside – sang along with some off-rhythm rock tune, and Quigley felt very old. He looked around the room; books, magazines, a TV, stereo CD player, all the stuff of a reasonably good life. *Comfortable* was how he might have described himself. And he slopped the drink down his throat and threw the empty glass at the TV screen.

The heavy cut-glass tumbler exploded against the screen, splintering the glass deep but not injuring the tube. Glass shards filtered everywhere; in the thick-piled carpet they winked in a yellowish light. She was in from the kitchen. She hit him with a cloth, somewhere about the back of his head, but he couldn't feel it. She tried to scratch his face, but he grabbed her wrists and held them, ready, very ready, to break them like dry twigs. You're a dry twig, he told her, and she spat in his face.

Melanie was in the living-room doorway screaming at them, begging them to stop. Quigley was trying to knee his wife in the stomach. They danced around the room grotesquely for a few minutes, then collapsed onto the couch. It came close, in a perverse way, to resembling an act of love about to happen. Quigley was on top of his wife and spitting into her face like a schoolyard kid, half-aware that someone stood in the doorway, that someone was screaming. When he looked up and saw his daughter Melanie, his wife took advantage of the lull in the spitting to tear a wrist free and grab Quigley by the balls. He yelled, felt an erection starting, couldn't understand any of it, ripped her hand free by the fingers and bent her thumb back until she roared with pain. Melanie thumped upstairs, hysterical now. Quigley suddenly jumped free of his wife, free of the couch. She lay there, her skirt up around her waist, her underclothes, slip, panties, in some sort of sensuous disorder, and she lay there looking at him. He stood up, his erection dwindling. He didn't know what to do, where to go, what to say next. Fuck you, he said. Fuck *you*, said his wife. They were both covered in each other's spit and their faces were red from exertion and some odd sort of passion that had entered the fight. It was not supposed to be there. It was indecent. But Quigley looked at his wife and his wife didn't move. At last he moved to the living-room door, closed it, turned the little silver key in the lock. When he got back to the couch, as he'd imagined, his wife's legs had opened a little wider and she was grinning at him. He undid his belt, unzipped his slacks, and his wife leaned forward and drew them down around his knees. He was hard and his heart crashed against his ribs like a hammer on an oil-drum. He slobbered over his wife's belly, then pulled her panties aside and drew himself into her. They went at it with all sorts of puffing and moaning and his wife came first, arching her back, one breathy shout. Quigley shut his eyes and came with a deep throaty groan which contained a great deal of embarrassment. He slipped out of his wife. And she settled herself and stood up without a word. Listen, she said then from the door as she unlocked it; that child is so upset. See what you've done? She'll never forgive you for treating her mother the way you do. And she *saw* you. She *saw* the sort of animal you are. Well, not for long.

And his wife left the room; he heard her pad upstairs to do some consoling. No one consoled Quigley. He sat on the edge of the couch with his trousers down around his knees and his flaccid prick hanging there in the air like something useless. He was tired and didn't feel like moving. Then he remembered where he had to be, the men who depended on him. He pulled himself together, washed his face, left the house. He hated his wife. He hated what she did to him.

He drove now through the town, watched lights come on in shop windows, couples huddle together against the chill, a thin-legged man in bells and cap swallow fire in a corner. He remembered how good, how comforted, he had felt earlier that day, driving away from the house, finding himself with his team again, the old thrust and shoulder-punch of camaraderie.

He drove through streets he had known all his life. He felt as if he was driving inside a cocoon, isolated from the world.

He fiddled about with the radio switch, gave up. A light driz-
zle washed across the windscreen. He turned on the wipers.
Their rhythmic slap lulled him. An elderly woman with a dog
crossed in front of him and he slammed on the brakes. She
didn't even bother to look his way. He cursed her and drove on.
All around him, new buildings reared up behind wooden construction facades, new shops glared out over the narrow pavements. His town was changing. There were whole streets you
could drive down now and not know where you were. It was
out of hand. Planning permission, the whole process, a puzzle
to most people. Who benefited from all of this? The high-rise
townhouses were forbiddingly expensive. No one called them
apartments any more. Or *flats*. More money than a man could
earn in half-a-dozen years. Well, a man like him. He felt angry,
driving and looking around. He felt dull and angry that everything was changing and he wasn't in line for any of it. Never
would be. He felt robbed, cheated. He felt this way a lot these
days. As if something he had owned from birth was being
dragged out of his grasp. By strangers. The world was full of
strangers.

He drove and wondered what his wife's lover was like. A
man with money, a professional man. He wondered about that.
A man of certainties. How clinical, he wondered, would his
wife be, choosing this new man? More discerning than she'd
been choosing *him*? It was the sort of thing you thought about.
What was he like in bed? Better? Probably. Not hard to be. He
thought of the shapes of his wife and another man humping
and he felt a sick movement in his belly. Not nausea, something
else, something cold and alive.

Where had they met, his wife, this man? No way of knowing. And there was little point in trying to work it all out, and
it didn't matter anyway. He felt tired, bruised. It was possible to
think too much. He remembered a girl he'd known at university. She had been scarily beautiful, at least to him. Tall, slim,
fair-haired, witty. She dated blokes with good cars, in the days
when no one he knew had a car. They had spoken to one

another now and then; he had never had the courage to ask her out. He was afraid of her, intimidated. But he had always known she had been the one. Had he won her, his life would have been different. *Bullshit.*

Leaving the searchers by the inlet, Quigley had wanted to go home, talk to his wife, something like that, though he didn't reckon anything decent was achievable. It had been something he had felt the need to do. Now he wasn't so sure. Should he move out? Should she? Should he start looking for a place of his own? What about their kids? All the explaining. Quigley didn't know what to do next. He thought of driving home, maybe finding *the other man* there, maybe bludgeoning him to death with some heavy object, doing the same to her. He thought of seeing them and being made to retreat like a whipped animal, her laughter – *their* laughter – in his ears as he drove off. Nothing was predictable anymore. Nothing had on its old familiar coat. Everything was something else. Anything was possible and nothing was.

So Quigley drove three, four miles out of the town, guilty now about when he'd get back to his party at the inlet, thinking about it all the time, but driving.

He drove until it was full darkness and he stopped at a roadside pub called The Three Fiddlers. An illuminated sign – depicting three leprechauns in green jackets and pointy hats, fiddling away and dancing ludicrously on a hillside road, psychotic grins on their faces – swung in the wet breeze, making a squeaking, unoiled sound. Quigley parked his car in the gravelly carpark. A few more expensive cars slumbered around him. A video camera watched him from high up on the wall of the pub. He danced a few insane steps of a makey-up jig on the gravel and gave the thumbs-up to the camera. He felt ridiculous, ashamed, thinking about it a moment later.

The Three Fiddlers was the sort of place, Quigley imagined, where a well-heeled boss took his pretty secretary for drinks and a meal – something with salmon – as a prelude to a fuck-session. When he got inside, the place was virtually empty. A couple of open-shirted, grey-haired executive types leaned on the wooden bar, but they had files of all sorts open in front of them and they were busy. Two middle-aged schoolteachery women gossiped in a corner. Quigley had never been in The Three Fiddlers before, which he thought about now. A big colour TV occupied a shelf behind the bar and the young barman was watching it, the sound turned way down. There was an odour of beer and cooking. Smartly-designed menus lay on the cubicle tables and sat open on the bar. Menus with little tassled strings hanging out of them. Quigley felt hungry but the food here was far too expensive. He thought about secretaries and illicit meals and humping someone new, a total stranger, one of the teachers in the corner, the one with leg showing to the thigh in black tights. But her face was caked in make-up and showed her age. She was fighting it and losing. Quigley sat up at the bar and ordered a double whiskey. Then he noticed the helmets.

There were dozens, perhaps hundreds of them, all types, sizes, all armies, all colours. They hung from the mock-Tudor ceiling and clung to the mock-Tudor walls like limpets or black malignant moles. Not a fiddle in sight in The Three Fiddlers. A couple of unfurled Manchester United scarves behind the bar, over the photographs of various players, all smiling, and one big one of the whole team; and all these helmets. German army helmets, First and Second Wars, US army helmets, British army, miners' helmets, with or without lamps, football helmets, several American leagues, cricket helmets, a relatively new thing, a crash helmet with a bad dent in the side, jockey helmets, the kind you wore under the funny coloured peaked cap, riot helmets. And a whole lot more.

Quigley had never seen so many helmets and couldn't understand it. He called the barman away from the TV, sipping at his glass for comfort. The barman back-stepped to him, never taking his eyes off the TV and the opening blows of a boxing match. Two young boxers jumped about and did very amateurish things without hurting each other. Quigley glanced at it, then remembered the helmets. I've never been in here before, he said to the barman. I was curious about the helmets, so many of them. He collects them, the barman said. Who? The owner. He's not here right now, but he'll be in about ten. I don't want to speak to him, Quigley said. I was just curious. Well, he's a sort of collector of antiques, the young barman said. But very few of these helmets are what you'd call antique. Well, said the barman, I only work here. He tried to laugh it off, tried not to be offensive. But he kept looking, arms folded now, at the TV. Quigley lit up a cigarette and offered one to the barman. I don't smoke, thanks all the same, the barman said. He must be mad to collect all those helmets, Quigley said. Was he in the army or something? No, not that I know of, said the barman. It seems a waste of time and money to me, Quigley said. I'm losing money on that bloke with the shaved head on the right, said the barman, nodding at the TV. The two boxers danced around in total silence.

Quigley understood the directionlessness of bar conversations. He had done his bit and now he shut down, drank his whiskey, watched himself in the bar's long gilt-edged mirror. There was a time to shut up. He drank, thought about where he should be and where he was, and ordered another. The Three Fiddlers started to fill up. The door would open and a cold rush of air would shove a couple, a single middle-aged man, a bunch of lads laughing and out-for-the-night, into its mocked-up atmosphere, its helmets, its Manchester United snugness. Quigley got up and phoned his wife. There was no reply. All the kids were out, too. Even Melanie. The name, he'd often thought, sounded dangerously close to *melanoma*. What a name for a kid. He had to argue the toss back at the bar about stewardship of his bar stool with a clean-shaven teenager. His girlfriend wore tight white jeans and when she turned away Quigley stared at her visible panty line. Well, he thought, who would be in here in the first place if he had that to take home? You had to be young and stupid to ignore something like that.

Quigley chided himself for his bitterness. He'd always known it was there, just hadn't often acknowledged it. He felt old. He got himself another drink and looked at his reflection in the mirror behind the bar. What looked back at him didn't impress him. There was a time, he told himself, when he'd had a way with women, a sort of awkward charm. His wife had found him irresistible. At least it had seemed that way. All those years ago. Or maybe she'd told him so in an unguarded moment. One of her very few. But he could remember times. He could not remember all the names but he could remember times, places, odd rooms. Quigley liked a woman who could shout when she fucked. It made him feel good. He thought about this and felt himself getting an erection, there on the bar stool in a slowly crowding pub. He looked in the mirror and saw how old and ugly he was and felt the erection dwindle. Well, he thought, you had your thoughts, dreams. He drank deeply.

Every time the front door opened, a blast of cold, wet air came in. Every time the door opened, Quigley would half-turn on his stool and look. He didn't understand why he did it, it was a sort of reflex. But he did it time and time again. Youngsters in leather jackets, denim jackets, jeans, expensive ugly footwear, girls in black tights, long-legged, smile-faced. The world belonged to people thirty years younger, or maybe a hundred years younger, it didn't seem to matter, he had no part in it anymore. He wondered how old his wife's lover was. Maybe twenty. Maybe twenty and randy twenty-four hours of the day, all shapes, positions, all sorts of things you had to be young to do. All that energy. He'd had it once. He could remember. He ordered another drink. This time he was aware of voices blurring and laughter, as if from the bottom of a very deep well, billowing all around him. Was this how you drifted away, finally? Getting drunk, detesting youth, being one place when you should be some place else?

He went out for a pee. In the gents, two men in suits and ties talked rugby while staring down at their pricks and pissing against the ceramic. Quigley had to stand behind them, feeling strange and outrageous, until one of them had finished. When he was finished, he decided as a deliberate act of something or other not to wash his hands. And he straightened his hair with a broken-toothed comb. Fuck the world, he said into the cracked toilet mirror. And its mother.

He stumbled back into the bar and the room moved. Suddenly it was all too hot, too crowded, there was no air. Nauseous and fatigued, Quigley left his cigarettes on the wet counter of the bar and took off for the front door.

Nothing felt right. He was too drunk to drive and he knew it. He got into his car and the dashboard lurched up at him. He pushed open his door and vomited whiskey all over one shoe and part of the car's meek carpeting. Then he wiped his mouth with the back of his hand and righted himself in the driver's seat; somehow he managed to swing onto the road without hitting anything. He drove very slowly, brought his face right up to the windscreen. He was driving like this for ten minutes before he realised that he hadn't turned on his headlights or his wipers. It was raining, a soft, persistent, cloudy rain. He wanted to go right up to his front door and when she opened it he'd smash her in the face and say There, that's for the pain and the young guy fucking you. That's for everything, no matter what it was. That's for the past and the future. That's for me and that's for you. He conjured up visions of his wife's face splitting in a bloody pulpy mess all over the place and realised that he'd drifted into the middle of the road. Cars honked at him furiously and headlights blinded him. This is the way it is, Quigley said to himself. Then he said it out loud: *This is the way it is.* And he felt better, determined, solid in his truths, all of that. He'd smash the whore's face in and walk away laughing. And if her stud was there he'd do for him the same way. Nothing to it. And no one would condemn him for it; she was a slut. That's right. He knew people. There were ways a thing got buried. He knew his town. No one fucked with Quigley. Anyone with any sense knew that. Except his wife. She needed reminding. Every now and then a man stood up for himself, got himself *back*. That was all he was doing, wasn't it? No one blamed a man for that. It was necessary. Once more Quigley dragged the slow-moving vehicle back on to the right side of the road. Once more lights dazzled his eyes. He drove for longer than he could measure. He drove in and out of infinities. He drove over cliffs and across rivers. He drove up and down mountains and finally came up to the front door of his house. A light was on in the front downstairs room. He turned off his engine. And stared stupidly, for now he had no will and no courage and nothing at all left to play with. He felt slow hot tears course down his blubbery face and he knew he was defeated fair and square. This was how you got defeated, sitting like this, drunk, in front of your own house, afraid to knock on the door. This was all you could do, then, just sit and blub and let the rain piss on the car roof and hope everything would miraculously wash away, get clean. But it wasn't as simple as that. No. No indeed. Not as simple as that at all. Sometimes there was just nothing left to do, no way of changing things, a vacuum that did not need to be filled. A process that did not call for reversing.

Quigley drove away from the house, searched with one hand for cigarettes in his pockets, along the dashboard, and was still searching as he turned a corner onto open road, forgot to stop, and winged with a heart-tearing wrench of metal the front of an oncoming truck.

Quigley felt himself being tossed to one side and then the car stopped and Quigley looked out of his shattered door window at the high windscreen of the truck. Diamonds of glass were all over his lap and in his hair. The engine of his car had stopped but the truck's motor growled over him like something out of a jungle. Quigley just sat there, heard the driver's door of the truck open, saw wooden planks unloosed and spilling from the side of the truck, saw the driver come over to him. He was a big man, but he looked scared and timid. Easy to deal with, Quigley thought. Then he thought of the cops. They'd be along for something like this. They'd have to be. And he was drunk. The truck driver's face looked into Quigley's. Are you hurt, for fuck's sake? the driver said. Quigley could hear the fright in the man's voice.

Fuck you, he said. Look where you're going. You came out in front of me, said the driver, you fucking drunk bastard. Fuck you, said Quigley and pushed at his door to get out. But the door was bent and jammed. You just sit there, the truck driver said. Don't you move and I'll get the cops and maybe an ambulance. I don't need a fucking ambulance, Quigley said. Fuck what *you* want, said the driver. I'm protecting myself here.

Quigley was overcome by a sense of something having gone terribly wrong. He got out of his car when they'd managed to prise open the door; he got out and went mumbling to the police car and then to the ambulance and he sat on the back step of the ambulance and let an attendant bandage a cut on his hand. He vomited onto the road. He saw lights all around him, on the road, in the sky, coloured lights, lights with authority. He wanted to weep but couldn't do it. He sat looking at his bandaged hand, looking up at the faces of policemen, the face of the truck driver as he pointed accusingly at Quigley's battered car. Quigley'd never felt as helpless in his life. There was something comforting about it, to be so totally out of control, to have the rocky acre of your life tended by strangers.

He rode in the back of the police car and said nothing at all. He'd kicked up like a hurt kid when they'd suggested he go to hospital; shock, overnight stay, observation, words that hurt him and frightened him. In the speeding police car he found the world a different place. He felt like a criminal and didn't care. Not at first. When they led him up the steps of the country police station and he realised he didn't know where he was, he found his voice.

The interview room was brightly lit and warm. One barred window sat high up in the wall. Quigley was left there, the door half-open, for half an hour. He was given heavily-sugared tea and told that a doctor would be sent for if he felt unwell. He said no thanks, he was fine, he didn't need a doctor. He needed a cigarette, ha-ha. No smoking, Quigley was told. Again a helpless feeling, but the comfort side of it was wearing off.

Quigley's world was wearing off; he was shedding it, or it was being stripped from him. He sat staring at the floor, all those cracked tiles, and felt unbelievably tired. Now and then he'd flashback into the earlier part of the evening and he had the vague and very unsettling notion that he'd murdered his wife and kids. He didn't know how, just that it was possible. Maybe he couldn't remember doing it but he'd done it all the same. Any moment now they'd come in and charge him with it. Then the dark thoughts would go away and he would see himself as just another drunk driver who'd caused an accident, and what was the worst they could do to him? No one was hurt; well, there was his scratched hand. But he couldn't be charged with that, after all. It was his own hand. He could see out through the half-open door into a sleepy office with a police-man typing at a desk and another one talking into a telephone. In the corner of the room a television spoke softly about tomor-row's weather. He could just about see the weatherman point-ing at a map. Then the door opened fully and a policeman came in. You are who you say you are, Mr Quigley, the officer said. Quigley looked at him. Maybe his wife was fucking a police-man. Of course I am, Quigley said. And I know people. I know the *head man*. Your top man. Is he around? I can explain all this. It was inexcusable, but these things happen, you know, women trouble, a few drinks, ha-ha. We have a different man in charge here, sir, if you wish to speak to him.

Quigley looked up at the fresh, youthful face of the officer as if he were an imbecile. Look, son, everybody knows Quigley, ha-ha. I'm in and out of police stations ten times a week. Half the time I *work* for the police. Everybody knows me, where to get me, what I do. Just make a telephone call and I'll have this cleared up in no time. I was silly, sure, but it's on my own head, isn't it? No one was hurt, but me, ha-ha.

Quigley held up his bandaged hand and waved it ridicu-lously in front of the police officer. The man looked at it and snorted. Quigley brought down his hand and realised how fool-ish he looked. The world was falling apart anyway, so what did it matter how he acted, what he said? Fuck pride. This was a strange police station and it dawned very quickly on Quigley that he wasn't going home. And he was scared. Scared of being locked in a room, scared of hearing the lock click and his jailer walk away, whistling. His heart began to pound and he wished to whatever was left of his personal gods that he had access to another whiskey. But at least a cigarette. He asked for one. The young policeman was getting him to sign papers. His hand shook. His signature was a scrawl. Help me, he said. Pardon, sir? said the policeman. Get me a fucking cigarette, for the love of Christ! But he no longer knew what he meant and it didn't matter anyway. He was watching the television, the advertisements for holidays in sunny places and fast new cars. He was watching impossibly young and beautiful girls shaving their legs. He was watching young and muscular men shaving their impeccable, flawless faces, half-naked women in silhouette in the background waiting to come out and fuck like mad. He was watching a world that some part of him really believed in flick and flash across the small square screen. So close, so far. If only he'd been born someone else or somewhere else. That was the real trick. To get out of being yourself.

But he was here, now, and the two policemen were getting impatient, or it appeared to him that they were. Crackling voices came over the police radio. The world went on with its petty crime and its fucking. He knew he'd survive the cell for the night and the court in the morning. He'd lose his licence, perhaps. Get off with a hefty fine, whatever. No jail. They wouldn't, would they? After all, no one had been hurt, nothing but his damned hand. Or maybe they were just trying to scare him so he wouldn't do it again. Cops played games, you knew that from books, magazines, every detective show on TV. They messed you around. But maybe he'd murdered his wife and his kids. Maybe they knew that now, too.

Then the worst thing in the world happened to Quigley. Worse than anything that night. He looked up at the little television and the late news programme was on. The older policeman turned up the volume and stood craning his neck up to where the TV was cradled on a ledge on the wall. Quigley knew why people killed themselves now. He knew what it was ended every single thing you had. He knew what withdrew all hope of redemption. He'd always known, perhaps, but Christ they didn't have to broadcast it on TV! They didn't have to show the world he was redundant, unnecessary.

Unnecessary. The word hung in the air, somewhere between Quigley and the rest of the living world. Up on the news programme one of his search party was giving an interview about finding the body of a young man in reeds halfway up the river an hour before. When he'd been in The Three Fiddlers or fucking about outside his own house or crashing into the truck. They'd been getting on with doing their job, their duty, and it was as if he'd never existed. Who the fuck needed Quigley? They'd searched and found the body and it was all over and Quigley was, well, wherever he was. No one spoke about him. He listened to the interview and the questions and answers and no one once mentioned his name. No one had missed him. No one needed him. That was how it felt when you stepped off a railway bridge and went into a cold inlet and got washed up a river. You had become unnecessary. That was what happened when your wife started shagging another man. Redundancy, pure and simple. When that happened, when you knew it was happening, it didn't matter whether you were in jail or in mid-air. What had gone before, what life had been a thousand million years ago when you'd been something, was wiped clean out of the accounts of things. So Quigley looked at the faces talking and trying to be solemn and yet glad to be on TV and hated them, at the same time knowing he was exactly where he should be right now. He'd stepped away from being like everybody else, like men who found corpses on rivers, all of that, a long time ago and it had taken until now to realise it and understand the full extent of that exile. He was in mid-air, falling, falling, not giving a fuck anymore and in a sort of way enjoying the breeze in his face and the prospect of drowning utterly.

They do a damned good job, those volunteers, said the policeman watching TV.

Who'd do it, eh? said Quigley. Take a special sort of man to do that sort of thing, look for dead bodies.

The policeman looked at Quigley as if he'd blasphemed. It takes balls, he said, a sort of accusation in Quigley's direction. And so you say you know people in town, Mr Quigley. Now, what sort of people would a lad like yourself know that might come searching for *you*?

The younger policeman started to laugh, a crude, mocking guffaw. Quigley looked from one to the other. He wanted to tell them the whole story, that he was the leader of the volunteer search team. All of that. But he wasn't the leader of anything anymore and he knew that only too vividly. He was fucked and they could laugh all they wanted to. He was their prisoner.

Don't worry, sir, the younger policeman said. Your wife is on the way over. She's been informed. But you'll still be our guest for the night.

That did it. Quigley started crying and he couldn't stop.

Rising Higher

Someday I'll write a book about it, about the smell. That dead smell of cigarettes and damp. Clings to your clothes. Jackets that sag, cheap denims that wrinkle and tear, shirts with sweaty dirt moulded into the collars. Shoes well down at the heels. And there's the dead laughter. In the queues. You try to crack jokes and look casual, bigger than at any other time of your week. Winks and nods, some sort of code imitating shrewdness. As if these dead shuffling men had anything in the world worth concealing. It's even quieter, sometimes, in the women's queue. That weight, that burden of apprehension the nearer you get to the pay-hatch. Maybe today is your day. Maybe today you've been discovered, your petty crime laid out for all to see. Now and then someone gets sent to the Supervisor.

The feeling that you could tear the world apart with your teeth, that God, as usual, has slipped out to another room. Butts of cigarettes. Anxiety always there, always. Up to the pay-hatch; is it permitted to joke with these pay-hatch people? A flaw in your claim form? No? You sign your name to a list of penalties and warnings. The entire State is waiting to swallow you up; a noose swings over every pay-hatch, so be warned. Nobody knows who hasn't done this, been here. There are a lot of smug bastards who think they know but they don't. First week or two on the dole, you still have spunk. You answer all the ads. You wait for replies, confident of getting something. Third week and first month, you feel less confident, as if you've been suffering from a wasting disease which has only now decided to make itself manifest. You try less often, you sleep half the day and get up feeling stunned. You get angry. You are always tired and fearful of you don't know what. By the end of the second month on the dole, you know God doesn't exist, which is like discovering a great secret, and you feel liberated in an odd way. You don't care about other people and you don't bother to look for work anymore. You get comfortable and walk with a stoop. Then there are the pubs. Some people get hooked on videos and watch blue movies one after the other half the day and all night. Don't tell me you know about this unless you've been there. Everybody looks as if they were just waiting for their case to come up; the machine works now to trap you and you are treated – in the bank, in shops when you look for Hire Purchase – like a criminal or someone who is about to commit a crime but hasn't made up his mind what kind. You don't bother with the clean shirt, the pressed pants, the fresh underwear and new socks. If you're married, the wife and kids are noises you learn to put up with; they can't ease what is going on in your head, the urge towards oblivion. Nothing has worked out as it was planned, as it was promised. Don't tell me anything unless you've been there. There are a lot of smug stupid bastards who think they know, and say they know, but they don't.

Alvarez had gathered a small group of trusted soldiers around him and struck out for the coast, or what he imagined was the coast, and in two years and seven months he had not arrived at the sea. By now his party were reduced to himself, the ship's cook who was known as El Gordo, the Fat One, and Juan, El Huso, so called because he was

*as thin, they said, as a spindle. But most likely it was because he had
a habit of humming vague songs and tunes as he worked. El Gordo,
the cook, was blue-eyed and devotedly catholic, in a way that his
captain, Alvarez Martinez Nunez y Nunez, native of Pizarro's
home-town, Trujillo, and himself a Catholic, did not understand.
Before preparing a meal, El Gordo said the Rosary. This prolonged
things irritatingly. None of them had eaten anything more than roots
and occasional mammals for an outrageously long time. Still they
had to endure El Gordo's Rosary. And he would insist on a prayer of
thanks after each meal. Neither Alvarez nor El Huso ever thought
there was much to thank God for. What God? they thought. God
played clever and stayed in Spain. Alvarez also suspected that El
Huso preferred men to women, but could prove nothing. Rumours
had reached his ears at sea. But that was a thousand years ago, when
he had a ship and a healthy, or reasonably healthy crew. Sometimes
El Huso saw painted faces in the trees, and at night El Gordo said he
saw white-winged angels flittering from tree to tree and bush to bush.
Alvarez scratched his beard and struck out for what he thought was
the sea.*

I read a lot but can't afford to buy new books so I peruse the
secondhand shops and now and then get lucky. Horror stories
are light reading when the day has given you nothing. Detective stories, Agatha Christie, when you've filled the gut three
times in the one day and have a packet of cigarettes home with
you. Don't anybody say he knows unless he's been there. Anyway, recently I picked up this book about these Spanish *con-
quistadores*. That's how you pronounce it in Spanish, I've been
told. The book is sheer escapism and great stuff, although if
you'd been there you mightn't have thought so. Alvarez, the
captain, has lost all his crew except a religious maniac cook and
a thin bloke who's probably gay, or something like it, but the
captain can't prove it. Not that it matters, because the rest of
the crew are dead or forgotten and the ship is disintegrating a
long way behind them. Alvarez is lost and thinks he can find
his way back to the sea. So he wanders on and on, getting

nowhere. What fascinates me is the visions. The thin bloke and the fat religious cook-freak think they see things all round them. Now I understand that physical degradation, hunger, exhaustion and illness, or a combination of these, can produce weird things like visions and singing and statues that move and this sort of thing. So I'm interested to know if, when a man is out of work for long enough and degraded for long enough and made to feel like shit for long enough, will he be subject to similar visions and auditory hallucinations. The book as it unfolds is like an album of photographs to me. Each page makes me imagine that I can see something that isn't there. At least, that humiliation might open doors. I've been feeling particularly humiliated since Jenny left me. Fuck her, anyway; but on the other hand I really liked her. Love on the dole is a phenomenon worthy of serious study. It is not like love in any other condition. Don't tell me you know if you don't. Lack of money means you can't go anywhere and that leads to tension because no one can sit in all day and stare into someone else's face and pretend it's fun. It isn't. When I met Jenny we did what most people do, which is fuck all day, although she hated me using that word and said she preferred to think of us making love. She'd put Beethoven on the record-player and blast out the Fifth Symphony bump-bump-bump-BUMP as we steered ourselves upriver. She had a nice two-roomed flat and a small black-and-white TV. I urged her, on her waitress' salary, to get a colour telly and a video. She couldn't afford them of course. We'd walk by the river, but the river stank in summer. Yes, we were together about a year, and winter, harsh and cold and full of shivering and huddling together with the 'flu under the thick blankets, finished us.

Spring came and we argued, about nothing much and about everything. We did not make love anymore and we did not fuck. Everyone's world depends on something and then dies when the thing it depends on runs out. For us it was tolerance. She could have endured anything but my intolerance of my own powerlessness. I tried to get work and they offered me government work-schemes which were tailor-made for the employer and gave the employee a few quid more than his weekly dole and no rights whatever. I couldn't do that. Jenny was only human and needed things, little outings, promises, surprises. I could give her none of these things. We argued frequently and I hated myself for it. I stayed away from her, let her down on dates. One night I got drunk and went back to her flat and it was locked up and I banged at the door until the landlady came down and told me she'd call the police if I didn't fuck off and the young lady was gone. I ended up that night in a fast-food place, formica tables and neon lighting and everything plastic, even the food. I was forcing paper-tasting chips down my throat and across the plastic knives and forks two young kids, dressed in designer jeans and thick-soled shoes and with their heads virtually shaved and both of them looking like clones of the other half-dozen shaven-heads at the counter, were chatting casually about getting their respective fathers to sign for a bank loan for them this summer as, ho- · hum, university life was such a drag and maybe America would be nice. Don't tell me you know anything about anger unless you've been there. I knew the world was bent when I heard this. I hated those teenagers more than I hated myself and God, and that's something. Listen to me: I felt my blood boil. I heard it thrumming in my ears. I knew that I was capable of wrecking the joint and if I'd had a machine-gun or even a sledge-hammer I'd have gone to work, I was mad enough. These clones didn't have a bother in the world, they dressed right, shaved their heads as if they were going into the Marines, swaggered around like they owned the place and knew nothing, absolutely nothing about life but acted as if they'd just invented it. I'd never been that cock-sure of anything even when I was their age and I hated them for it now. Spoiled bastards, I thought. Give you a couple of years on the dole and you'd smarten up. But nobody smartens up on the dole. That's not what the dole does for you. It does not make you a man. It robs you of manhood. But that wasn't the way I was thinking, looking at the clones. I swear one of them was going bald and he couldn't have been more than nineteen. What happened to the hippies? I consoled myself that it was better in the days when I smoked shit and wore my hair long; Dylan, Hendrix, that scene. The clones left. I went home, sick, angry, disappointed that I wasn't dead.

El Huso spoke in his sleep. He laughed in his sleep. When he awoke he could remember nothing of his dreams. Alvarez, unable to sleep under his covering of large leaves one night, listened intently as The Spindle spoke at great length in a language unknown to Alvarez, who had a smattering of Latin and could read and write. One night El Huso startled his captain and the cook by breaking from his sleep with a scream, as if leaping overboard from a stricken ship. He said that God was a frog and had appeared to him in his sleep and tried to drag him into his mouth with one flick of his long sticky tongue. Sweating, El Huso fell back into slumber. But Alvarez and El Gordo were disturbed. Fatigue and hunger had destroyed the captain's sense of logic and common sense. He fell to praying alongside his cook, a mumbled, half-remembered litany of Aves and Credos. Let it be said that Alvarez Martinez believed in nothing above the earth or in the earth. But he prayed to shut out visions of a jungle-bidden frog-god with a sticky tongue who swallowed men while they slept. In the morning, when El Gordo went collecting sticks, he found that they had made camp beside a shallow pool, green-coloured, slightly smelly, but full of fat listless frogs, a dozen or more of which he killed with a stick and carried back for breakfast.

It's often a question of eating the other bloke before he eats you. I've always believed this. Today, dole-day, I have money. I owe money. I walk from the dole office to the bookmaker's and ask for the proprietor, a fat Northerner who made his money working on building-sites in London before coming home to set up this place. As usual, loafers and dole-heads are hanging around the racing-sheets that sway like lists of war-dead on the walls. Frankie would bar me from the place or make a public spectacle of me in the pub if I didn't pay up. I owe him five quid, peanuts. But for this he would make me suffer his particular brand of public humiliation which would be worth more than five pounds to him. Losing an eye has made him a sadist. A canister of liquid something blew up in his face and took out his eye and gave him many thousands of pounds to add to the bread he'd made breaking his back for years humping bricks. Frankie never married. Hadn't time, I suppose. Fifty and a whiskey drinker. An eye-patch, always tartan green, God knows why. I walk into the bookmaker's and no one turns to see who is coming in because no one cares. If I was writing about this, I would not fictionalise it by saying there was some kind of great buddy-thing with the boys on the dole. A few words exchanged on the steps and that was it. No, money makes you impatient, but you can't say for what. And in the bookie's, everyone is in that agitated state, that anxious overblown cigarette-smoke state of being which is all they can manage of enjoyment. The Big One. Maybe today's the day. But the only winner is patch-eyed Frankie. Women at home with no money for food. Frankie doesn't care. Why should he? He's not a charitable organisation, is he? Are *you*? No. Right. Then you see what I mean. On the dole you quickly learn that chatting up somebody is a waste of time unless they're good for something. So no one says much in the bookie's, which is dole-people territory.

Frankie is seated like a fat frog behind the three-bar grille of his office, always alert, always suspicion glowing out of that one eye. I thrust a five-pound note through the bars. Thanks for that, I say, in wink-and-nod language. Fancy anything today? Frankie asks me, meaning the runners. I haven't even bothered to look at them, I tell him. He sniffs. The eye-patch tartan, I notice, is criss-crossed with tiny threads which may well be of fine spun metal and capable of carrying messages, instructions, on a thin current; maybe his eye has been replaced by a computer of some sort. But he resembles nothing so much as a fat repugnant god seated in a sacred niche. I realise that I actually see him as this, that I see his blood-sucking menacing horrible actuality, and I want to laugh in his face or spit in it. Take a look at the three-fifteen at Lincoln, the fat god says. Frankie is asking me to read some sacred scripture. Not today, I say, and walk out of the bookmaker's office hardly able to breathe, I am so angry and tired, suddenly. Tired, yes. I get tired easily, thinking, trying to get through, or make sense of it. I once knew what my life was about and what I had coming to me and what I could work at and make better and what was useless and ready for throwing out. But none of that clear-thinking knowledge is possible anymore. My life has become a series of experiences which have been jotted down hastily and filed away; or a group of colourful but valueless paintings. Once I kept a diary, but when Jenny left I read over it and found that it was, essentially, the journal of an out-of-work semi-drunk, and the realisation that I had written it scared me to death. I burned it, a private ritual. I tossed what was left of it down the jacks. I have never had anything even remotely interesting to say, write about, add to the world's store of knowledge. The diary of a man on the dole is a list of repeated rituals. Who wants to read that? Crap. I never write letters. Who would I write to? Who would answer? Rain crept into the sky as I left Frankie's, the drab corpse-grey sky of dole-day. I walked up the main street and went into the post-office and purchased a lottery ticket. I made out my numbers, blocked them off, handed in my pound. With my lottery numbers on the precious receipt, I strolled to the door. Feeling lucky, I walked back, asked the bloke if I could use the same card and mark out two more sets of lottery numbers. Certainly, he said. I blocked off the numbers, handed him the card and another pound; he inserted the card into the register to get a receipt and it went hay-wire. I'd forgotten to block out the two sets of numbers that I'd already chosen as VOID. Now two sets the same had been entered in the national game. Christ! He looked like a man stricken with paralysis. It took two phone-calls and a lot of sweat to put the business right. Having money had brought madness with it.

The sky was a greedy pale colour and down low over everything as if sucking everything up, street, people. The rain had

turned into a fine mist that soaked you. Shop lights creaked
and dimmed. The affair in the post office shakes me up a bit. It
is as if I had almost jammed the wheels of some massive
machine. The responsibility is enormous. I'm given to quick
flashes of paranoia and this is one of them. I walk and feel helpless, lost, scared, and there are people all around me who know
my crime. Everything has become transparent. Nothing holds.
I am wet and miserable, but that's only words. You have to
know about it. I have tried to spend my money to make more
money and chaos has been the result. A sign, surely, that I am
forbidden to try to raise myself up, to improve things even by
chance. I long to get back to my book and the comfort of silent
reading. I am hungry. But I am afraid that if I sit down at a café
table I will disintegrate. If I eat, people will stare at me. The
thought of bringing something back to cook at my flat fills me
with weariness. Everything is conflict, I cannot think of anything without being plunged into unwholesome dilemmas. I
see girls going by and I look at their backsides and I feel edgy
and randy. So I buy a tabloid newspaper, disappear into a public house jacks like a thief, open up Page Three and start to
masturbate. The jacks is underground, under the street, and
even as I do what I'm doing people's feet crash over my head.
When it's over I feel nothing but guilt and emptiness. I leave
the paper behind the cistern and pass through the pub with a
look on my face that tells them I've planted a bomb downstairs.

*Alvarez Martinez, soaked to the skin from pushing his way through
hanging vines, thick water-laden leaves and the fine mist of the jungle, began to edge towards the understanding that he was irretriev-
ably lost. He did not want to admit the thought, conscious still of a
need, probably absurd at this stage, to keep up morale. His legs lifted and came down as if they had weights attached to them. Leeches
cling obstinately to his face, despite vicious swipes of his hands. El
Huso has begun to sing, a tuneless rhythmic thing which keeps rough
pace with Alvarez's legs pumping up and down. The captain becomes
uncomfortably aware that the The Spindle is right behind him. El*

Gordo, somewhere off to his right, curses God and strikes with his blunted sword at tantalising vines. There is something healthier in that sound than in El Huso's cacophony. Eventually the Trujillo captain, heir to the courage and obstinacy of Pizarro, stopped and turned to El Huso. What are you singing, man? I don't know its name, said The Spindle. Where did you get it? God knows, El Huso said; but it won't leave my head. It is a horrible sound, said Alvarez Martinez; it doesn't seem to me that it could ever have been a proper song. Perhaps so, said El Huso; perhaps my mind has made it up and it comprises all the horrors in my mind and their sounds. There is a hint of arrogance in that answer, said Alvarez. I don't intend to be arrogant, my captain, said El Huso; but I thought a song would ease our way a little. A song might, indeed, said Alvarez; but not whatever it is you're mouthing. Do you wish me to stop? El Huso said. Of course not, Alvarez replied. If it is all we have then sing it! Stepping back, Alvarez stumbled. El Huso jerked forward, arms outstretched, to save his captain from falling over. At that moment Alvarez had the uncomfortable sensation of passing straight through the seaman and landing face down in the brambly wet undergrowth. Lying there, he heard El Huso singing.

You know what I mean? Some things you can't make up. I once watched a huge white swan coming up out of the river and lighting down on a child in his pram. The mother went bananas. The swan flapped up and away and the child didn't even cry. There was something magical about it. It happened in the middle of the day and maybe I was the only one who noticed. But the image stayed with me for a long time. I felt sort of privileged. Maybe these little secrets come out all around us all the time and we don't have the time to see them, rolling along as we do, unstoppable. Makes you think there's something going on but it's got nothing to do with a grey-bearded grandfatherly old man peering down from the clouds. Makes you think there's an order to things, even if for most of the time we're outside it. The bloke who wrote this book I'm reading, I know nothing about him. The covers of the book were gone, and the first few pages, when I bought it. You take your chances in a secondhand bookshop. But he had a vivid imagination, if that's what it was. Or maybe he had access to old manuscripts from Spain. Who knows? I pass by a butcher's shop. A smiling pig, standing up on his hind feet, wearing a butcher's hat, looks out at me. A bus goes by, exhausts busted as usual, and makes a very loud angry sound as if it were in pain. There's smoke all over the place, dark and thick. Outside a fast-food place there's a polar bear handing out leaflets advertising free ice-cream for kids. Some things you can't make up. I don't think anything in that book is made up. I think they all happened, even the weirdest things. Only the shapes and appearances have changed. There's a magazine lying open in the drain. The cover shows an ancient peasant from some place in Asia screwing his eyes up at the camera. I step on his face. Who knows, but somewhere in Asia an old peasant might suddenly find himself crushed under a gigantic boot? Tell me it is *not* possible, and then prove it isn't.

I look up and down the street and know, the way I *know*, that there are many things in life I will never enjoy and many more I will never see or experience. I believe that going mad begins with this. Then the river seems attractive. Am I exaggerating? Definitely not. Maybe there's peace in resignation. Accepting your lot. But what if even your lot rejects you?

I go in to my usual pub. Taped musak, the worst mechanical kind, soft watery voices and pleas to come home. Where's *that*? My mates aren't in here yet; too early. I call them my mates but we don't share much. Most of the time we are in the same place getting pissed together and cracking dirty jokes. We reach a point where we think we can screw filmstars and most women who come in. What would you do *there*? Look at that ass. This sort of shit. Outside it's still daylight and we're eye-fucking all over the place. By the time everyone else is coming home from a day at the office, we're usually drunk and melancholy. No woman will come near us, we know that. They're all quite safe, too. Knowing we won't be going anywhere with anyone tonight, we usually console ourselves that sleeping with people is, these days, dangerous. If we were sober we'd probably be foolish enough to try. Drunk, we're better off. That's some logic, but there it is. Over everything, the musak, the tinkle of glasses, the barman's superior weight. Two Chinese blokes came in. They were dressed immaculately. I can still see them. They ordered beer, sandwiches, kept themselves to themselves. When they left, I asked the barman where they came from. China, he said. Rain began to lash the windows. I began to feel sorry for myself, as if that was something new. I longed for Jenny. I thought I remembered her 'phone number; that is, her parents' place. Was it two-one-something, or three-one-something? Or three-one-two-something? I fumbled a couple of coins into the box and dialled. It was a wrong number and then I got all confused and gave it up. I went back to the bar, to my pint of German lager. A young mother had come in with two kids and one of them, a boy about eight years old, had rushed up with great enthusiasm and knocked over my drink. It dripped solemnly onto the floor. The barman looked at it, smiled, looked at me. I'll put on another one, he said. I couldn't say anything, but smiled stupidly at this little boy whom I wanted to flatten under an enormous boot. The boy was the barman's son, as I instantly acknowledged, and even my anger was useless. Well, it usually is. Except that once. When was that, now? Time goes all over the place. Eventually, though, I remembered. I remember now, for what good it does me.

I live and die in this place, I am resurrected here, I sail with a sharp diamond-like splendour over the thick red carpets, along the white-tiled lavatory hall, and I pee with golden certainty down the white cliffs of porcelain, a liquid emotion. I am all the waterfalls of the world. I distil the essence of alcohol and blood. I return to my throne high above the rest of mankind. I rest one arm on the wet wooden top of the bar and time flutters away like a terrified bird. Raw, the soul, as night comes. I am all violence in harmony, a symphonic lustful time-bomb, a shout preparing itself. The women come and go, festering in

my eyes, gaudy, jewelled, smiling desperately. Smoke is everywhere. Voices form a worldess, shapeless wall of sound. No one
communicates. Everyone is suddenly made dumb. Noise only.
I drink, feel the liquid salvation slide down my throat like
merciful rejuvenating phlegm. I am dying of myself. Outside, in
the morning, the wasteland of absolute reality will reassert
itself; is it possible to live there any longer? The world is full of
frogs. Is it so unusual, therefore, to feel so alien, so different? An
empty potato-crisp packet bursts between the palms of a manic
joker, a drunken good-fellow. Ha-Ha-Ha-Ha. Quick; I toss the
bomb among the tables. Soon there will be total silence, only
the hiss of granulated concrete falling like powdered snow. I am
afraid to go home, to leave, and I heartily wish I could bring
this world down around my neck. I am no one; how many people can say that? Ha-Ha-Ha-Ha. I get sick all over myself in the
jacks and wash my face and reassemble myself for the walk
through the bar and in the street the cold air hits me like a
whore's kiss. Taxi? No. I decide to walk. Strenuous but healthy.
Past the fast-food take-aways with their dead-sausage and
dying-burger odours and the defeated lonely empty terrified
faces of old men in corner seats chewing chips and chicken and
staring, Christ, forever staring, at the street beyond the window.
I turn up the collar of my wasted tweed jacket. How much
money have I spent? How much money is there in the world?
Well, I have spent all of it. In the pub. All. Fuck you, I declaim
with every seeping rain-sodden step. Fuck you and fuck you.
Whoever you are. I am the dead-still midnight, the stalking
dead-weight something-you've-forgotten. Curse these streets;
shops with their doors closed, their windows lighted, man-
nequins dressed in expensive shoes, expensive coats, wearing
plaster smiles of gratitude to the god who designed them. Who
could not be grateful for such clothes, such smiles? By the railings of the park some men in dark coats are cruising one another, up and down, slowly, approaching, offering the obligatory
ritualistic cigarette. What do they talk about, to break the ice?
They are always here, going round and round like those cast-

iron figures on huge German public clocks, in-and-out and round-and-round. Rain on tree-leaves. Taxis that glitter like eggs encrusted with diamonds. Above it all, the huge spires of churches, like upturned compasses scraping the belly of the sky, young couples who cannot yet feel the rain, who laugh and splutter at everything. Whiff of Turkish tobacco; would I have a light? Fuck off. I only wanted…

Remember this, friend. I do not care what you only wanted, or ever want, or will want in the future. I wish you were dead. I care nothing for you. That is how I survive. Speak to me about God and I will show you the holes in my only pair of shoes. Don't mess with me or I will exchange my native brand of English for Americanese, slum-lingo, ghetto hip jive-talk man, and I'll tell you what I believe you should do with yourself. Upstairs, man, in my place, to hell with Brooklyn! The wife calls him a whoremaster every Friday night–Saturday morning and then the crockery goes and the child screams. Light your own cigarette. This is a free country, and I'm free to refuse you.

I am so angry I could weep. I want to sit down. I walk over the bridge. A small knot of people, a lump, dark under the rain, around the parapet, leaning over. Then heavy searchlights. For the moment I am taken up with what's going on, I cannot think of the cancer of myself on the body of this dilapidated world where I am stranded. Frogs everywhere, I said.

Alvarez Martinez, Captain, could not remember doing it, but when it was accomplished he felt unbearably alone, and the jungle crushed him, moved in on him, sniggered. El Huso had pissed himself – he was not much of a man, after all – and tried to say something before the knife had slashed, with one arced sweep, his jugular and blood had rained on the fat leaves and the crackling twigs. It was all very quick, done as Alvarez Martinez, sick to his heart of singing and the sound of another human being so close behind him, had decided to do it, in the same instant. Alvarez did not discuss it with himself. He wiped the long-bladed knife on his doublet and listened, now, for El Gordo. The man plodded like a mindless animal, without singing, without lust for company, without any knowledge of where he was going, through endless days and nights of jungle. At night, now, they were subject to the sounds of a chiming church-like bell, the location of which they could not discover; El Huso dead, El Gordo remained. Then, Alvarez felt certain, the aching bells would go away. They were attracted, demons, to the weight of flesh these men carried. The bells fed on them like blow-flies. El Gordo, when his time came, put up a fight, but eventually Alvarez, scratching at the man's face with both hands, had bitten deep into El Gordo's throat and torn it out as effectively as if he had developed lycanthropy. El Gordo wore that now familiar stupefied stare, and tumbled, fountaining, to the undergrowth, where he twitched largely for a while before subsiding. Now the jungle sent up a celebratory screech which deafened Alvarez of Trujillo. His heart pounded, but he was not afflicted with grief. He wiped his mouth with his doublet, as he had wiped his knife on his doublet, and strode off, alone, into the jungle, feeling and acknowledging the weight of loneliness but not having any doubt as to its snugness. So great was his hatred of all mankind at this point that Alvarez had forsaken emotion for a bleak self-confidence, such as is given to idiots or the incurably insane. God Himself sniggered behind the trees and it was He who rang that infernal and still present bell each night, as if to taunt Alvarez towards Hell through even more deplorable conduct. The bell was attracted, Alvarez conceded, not to El Huso or the dithering El Gordo, but merely to himself. It was seeking him out, perhaps over many miles of unthinkable God-weary darkness, driven by God but directionless until it had sniffed him, there, a furtive monkey jabbering (now) to himself in the jungle. Alvarez ate roots and insects and masturbated like a lunatic and yelled his mother's name (Maria Concha Martinez-Nuñez) out loud and then spat loudly on the jungle floor. He screamed that he shat on the world, and on everything else. Everyone in the world could kneel and kiss his behind. His monkey's behind. He screamed and imitated high notes of apes and clapped his hands and forgot, mercifully, about El Huso and El Gordo, wiped their memory out completely with a rage so pure and uninhibited that it was some time before Alvarez Martinez, who was rumoured to have known Pizarro when *a boy but who hadn't, came to the understanding that he had chopped off his left hand when it had tried to strangle him. Pain and death ceased to have meaning for him. He died often and was often in great pain, but none of it mattered. It seemed so naturally to accompany him that he could not imagine life without pain, without death, as constant companions. Then he understood that El Huso's real name had been Pain, and El Gordo's, Death, and that he had done well to put them in their respective places and conquer them. It all began to make sense. And it was comforting. And Alvarez Martinez Nuñez y Nuñez was only dimly aware of stepping, then falling from the jungle down onto a wind-blown sandy beach where a group of well-fed sailors, their ship bobbing peacefully a mile off-shore, were busy about the rape of a native girl they'd sequestered. Indeed, the girl had been truly confiscated, as they had every intention of killing her once they'd had enough, and, since she had at first appeared to go willingly with the sailors, her tribe would not have her back. Alvarez knew none of this as he became a man for an instant and threw up his arms. Unluckily for the captain, he became a man rather too convincingly, and when the busy sailors looked up they beheld a somewhat ragged but nonetheless very agile captain, braids and hose tattered but recognisable, leaping towards them. Fearing questions, rebukes, even punishment for what they were about with the girl, they whispered among themselves for an instant, which Alvarez took to mean they were trying to recognise him; and as he took one more leap which landed him, a wretched, starved, mad-eyed, one-handed, monkey-in-doublet figure, at their feet, the sturdiest among them, the cook, took off his head with one energetic sweep of his cutlass.*

So. They're dragging the river. A girl. Mutter-mutter in the rain, odours of damp clothes and cigarettes. No names. All very anonymous. Jenny is a dream and I cannot remember when was the last time I dreamed her. Fluttering of hair, a laugh, a scream, my throat torn out. I'll feel better than this shit. I look upriver and the searchlights probe like fingers under a skirt, that unequalled exquisite pungent darkness. A monstrous ship, sails jumping in the wind and rain, is born on the black crazed surface of the river. It slips its moorings, drifts out into the crawling fingerhold of night. I stare into its rigging, see the immutable logarithmics of ropes and knots. The timbers creak, a bird like a shot of silver round its bows. Searching, the searchlights hover. In my pockets, a half-full packet of cigarettes and a box of damp matches. My feet swim in my shoes, soggy, feverish. Figures melt into the water. Shouts. Nothing definite, the night and river black together like a conspiracy of darknesses. I know I will be safe between the covers of the book; safe, untouchable. Drowning, I swallow a lungful of minnows. Above me, seagulls clear their throats and sway on the upcurrent. Jenny. Hair loose in the water like some kind of weed. To Hell with this, the crowded parapet, the searchlight, the night. I'm aboard, now. Let me be. Back, back under the covers, my fingers gripping my flaccid penis as if it might get away, and the familiar smells of home, cigarettes, bad feet, and rain against the window. Nothing lasts forever. I told Jenny that. You don't know, if you haven't been there.

The Artemis Concerto

So. Grain after grain, running through, tickling. Salt and the
dust of mountains, or so many glittering worlds cascading, each
individual, correct, perfect. My toes, naked, in the sand; my fingers filtering. The grain of the wooden planks, the stubborn
throb of waves. Sunlight as soft as a man's hand. I am sleepy.
But luxuriously so. I could wade into sleep and drown in it,
happily. When I close my eyes, there is the gentle redness of filtering light. Down on the beach they are running, I hear their
shouts, laughter. I wait, patient sentinel, seated like a figure in
a painting on the harsh rugged boarding of the porch, the
breeze beneath my skirt, on my dry cool thighs, my legs spread,
while the world opens and closes like a valve around me. When
I open my eyes I see them against the certain influx of waves,
white flesh broken by the colours of their bathing costumes.
They are running away from me, towards the edge of the world.
Her hair, my sister's hair, longer than mine, leaps out behind
her like a dull bronzed flag. He takes her in his arms, moulds
her breasts with his hands; even at this distance I can feel that

moulding. And I take a cigarette, light it, feel the rough unpleasant hastening of the heart. Behind me the second movement of Beethoven's Ninth comes to an end; I tread barefoot across the splintery planking, in to the dark pleasure of the house, turn over the record, set the needle carefully in the groove. My eyes adjust to the comfortable gloom. On the porch, the sun cuts a triangle of immense bright power. The flowered curtains sigh and I blow grey-blue smoke over the infinite spaces between the items of furniture.

(They walked back to the green-painted house. The wooden bungalow, with reluctance, the sea had been so warm, the sunlight hard and friendly, like a slap on their tender shoulders, the back of their legs, and now the walk through the sand and sparse grass back to the cool deliberateness, the open tiresome hospitality of the house was proving simply too much of an effort, a duty. No. To lie in the occasional dunes, to caress the thigh, the moist lip, urge on the strangled cry; besides, the house meant a clamouring silence. She walked around the place with an utter silence which bore down on them both like a weight. I know what she needs, he'd said. What you're getting plenty of. Stubbing out cigarettes in the sand. Wait a minute, there's something in your eye. Sand gets everywhere, and don't I know it. Show me. Show me where the sand is and I'll clear it. Stop. No chance. There's something hurting my back. Now. That's better. We have time. No rush. Take your time. Is that OK? And let it all start all over again, the nagging aching push downwards, and her fingers down the back of his trunks. O Jesus, O Jesus, the way you make me *feel*! And he could hear, even with the blood beating his ears to bursting, the music pouring out of the house mischievously, as if she'd planned it, rising, up, up, over them like a blanket; all that way back to the house and you could still hear the damned music. Jesus, the *way* you make me *feel*! Her fingers played beneath the elastic of his trunks and his face puckered and that was that. There is always a great expulsion of air from the mouth. Then a warm sweet desperate need to sleep. All the way over the sparse, brittle, bent-under-the-breeze grass, blade-sharp, that stuff, there is the sound of Beethoven. In his trunks, the hardness reluctant to leave. Her face beetroot red. The house drawing nearer in proportion to the sea's withdrawal from them. Now she'll have a white cloth on the table and a bottle of cheap red wine and she'll smoke as she serves the salad, crisp, frightening, green and drenched in vinegar. He stopped, bent down, kissed her sand-filled mouth, pushed his tongue into her mouth and felt her teeth bite down gently. The way you make me feel. This is it. Your sister's bungalow by the sea. A weekend. If I were here alone with your sister we'd be the very best of friends. O yes we would. The legs. Thirty-odd. The way she stares sometimes. Then smiles. It's all friendly. O yes we would. Kiss me, promise you'll never leave me. Never, never, never. Breeze drying the sand from the flesh, stripping a layer of dead skin from the bone. There's something in her, your sister. Something that drives the knife in; I can feel it. I can feel it cut me, but you don't know anything about it. When I enter you I enter her, sometimes. My secret.)

The door swings open on the sea. A boat, sail untidy in the wind, drives along the horizon's thread. The table is immaculate. White cloth, bottle of red wine uncorked with the light playing through the wine and puppeting a handful of gleaming reflections on the cloth, wicker basket of French bread sliced up in convenient rounds, salad in a huge and heavy smoked crystal bowl, Beethoven on very low, the words of Schiller; gleaming too the knives, forks, spoons, polished and squeaky-surfaced the thin-lipped cups; delicate and almost invisible the stems of the wine glasses. Thin even slices of tongue and ham; she serves, leaning over the table and her breasts, small and visible, like a light breath. His eyes on me, don't think I haven't noticed. Tinkle of metal against earthenware; you have blue eyes, his were brown. Did you tumble my little sister in the sand-dunes? Fool if you didn't. She has sand in her hair, everywhere. And she smells salty; so do you. *There.* Those fingers of yours, how deep do they probe? Now they bend around a leaf of lettuce, my sister's scent dissolving in vinegar.

They ate, and she heard, or listened to, the irritating metal-lic ping of his fork against his lower teeth, and now and then it sounded like a scraping noise too, when he withdrew his fork and simultaneously pulled off a scrap of meat. A sound that would not go away. She seemed to hear every sound he made while eating; chewing, slipping the food down his throat, a litany of irritation. Disgusting, too, if you were to dwell on it. Her sister raised her full wine glass, spilled some wine on the white cloth, where the stain grew and bloomed like a rose. Not the neatly ordered roses of flower-shops, but the eager wild-petalled wind-broke things which sprout irrationally from graves and hedges. You drink too much, and you drink too fast, but it's not my job to reprimand you. You remember him, don't you? He wanted to take me to Louisville, Kentucky. On the banks of the Oh-High-Oh. He played the classical guitar and said that there wasn't a decent place in Louisville where he could obtain sheet-music and did I know a place? I did. We held hands. He hired a car, drove with me to a bed-and-break-fast in the country, I screamed and screamed from pain and the agony of achieving him inside me. And I wrote and he wrote and then we stopped.

The wine-level in the bottle lowered. He handed out ciga-rettes. She accepted, feeling the biting mellowness of the red wine on a lightly filled stomach, feeling the nicotine. He leaned back on his chair, bare legs, pullover careless over the swim-ming-trunks, hairy legs. Shyness at the breakfast-table; the landlady had carried the smell of cheap scented soap in among the tender toast-racks; and will you both be going to America now? They exchanged looks, not shy this time, confident as anything they were not going to America. At least not together. She had found it so painful that morning to look at him and so reassuring to know that no promises would be made. He had brown eyes, a scar on his knee, called her name out when they made love, long before he was finished, her name, like a mantra. His sweat and her own sweat. Nectar, to fill her tongue's hollow with the sweat along his spine.

Her sister stood up, jeans on now, hair full of sand still but tied up. She walked to the uneasy door and closed it shut. Getting chilly, she said. Those cigarettes are terrible, make me want to puke. Well, just don't puke all over the bloody table. The wine stain won't come out, you know that. Damn the wine stain, her younger sister said. Framed in the shut door. He, leaning his chair back on its hind legs, smoking, watching her, said smiling: It's not the cigarette, it's the wine, she can't hold her drink. As if he had conquered her finally, not enough he'd opened her like a tin of beans on their second, or was it their third date. She was looking at the flaring red tip of the cigarette and her jeans, tight between her sturdy legs, rippled as she adjusted her weight from one foot to the other. Christ, the last time we went out for a decent piss-up you had to be carried into a taxi. My father says any man who can't hold his booze isn't a man at all. So what does that make you, eh?

Slut. My sister has the makings of a slut, a good one. Well able to look after herself. The bed-head used to bang remorselessly against the wall. I would shut my eyes tight and bring my legs up for better thrust. This little house creaks when the wind blows. And the cigarettes are dry, stale. The table is like a battleground, everything destroyed that was once so neat, so planned, arranged. No music, record over. Only the sound of his chair on the boards, the arcane clickings of the bungalow, the distant sea. I became so well able to construct my body around his that I do believe we were one person at times and he'd taken me as raw as could be. One whole summer. When it was over, he simply, and quite rightly, went back to his wife. Who will help me with the dishes? Or will I leave them there until some other time, some vague place in the future? Will the spirits of this house tidy things away while we sleep? If only it were that easy. If only.

(Feeling the chair creak under him, he smokes lazily. Sensing more than seeing the girl off to his left in the doorway, and beyond her the sure slide of the sea. Her sister stands up, slightly away from the table, and lifts things; the empty wine bottle, a cup, a bowl; and the cigarette dangles obscenely from her lips. Ash floats to the floorboards. He rights his chair, stands up; to hell with this. The wine-and-nicotine cocktail spices his blood. He stands up. The waves sang, of foundered ships, drowned sailors, cargoes lost forever. He smiles at her, she drops her arms from the doorway, her glass is empty. One arm slips around her waist, she moves in to him. He can hear the softness, saltiness, slyness of the evening, a honey-colour in the light outside on the wooden porch, something tired and sensuous about the world which infects him. Behind him, sounds of things being cleared away, hidden. He sticks his tongue behind her ear, brings it down around the lobe, hears the purring in her throat. Outside on the wooden porch the evening wind is singing. I should help her with the washing-up, she says into his ear. Keep doing that and I'll crumple up on the floor. Now I could live with that, he says, mimicking a line he heard some American actor say on a TV series; live with that. He hears the phrase and it sounds alien in his own mouth; wash my mouth out with salt. Instead he goes into the shell of her ear with his tongue and tastes the sharp bitterness of the wax. If I yelled I'd deafen you, he says; then moves away from her. You often do, she says, pushing him even further away. Now; I'm going to help her dry or something, I feel bad, standing here while she's working. Off she moves, he stands in the doorway and watches her move. When I yell in her ear I deafen her, he tells himself; well, it takes a man to shout like that. He smokes the last of the cigarette and opens the door; immediately the unholy beauty of the evening hits his face, brings tears to his eyes, makes him want to run, shout, cry. He throws the stub into the sand, but before it can rest the wind takes it and drives it rolling hundreds of miles away into the crisp enveloping darkness. A moon, Jesus Christ! a moon the size of an orange, slipping up out of the sea; no, it comes up like a coin held between the lip of the sky and the lip of the sea; it is so beautiful, it makes him think he is bleeding, the sacrament of evening, the rust-hammered coin, upwards slowly into the blueblack night. The sea whispering beneath it all; he walks down onto the sand, feels the sand blast on his skin, the cooling sand. He pushes the bungalow behind him into its own massy darkness and walks towards the sea. The sand is damp, then sluggish and wet. By the time I get back the washing-up business will be over. But this is beautiful, really beautiful. He wants, for one moment, to throw himself upwards and into the evening like a spark from a fire. Instead he lifts a stick, a twisty scrap, and digs out I Love You to no one in particular on the wet sand, and he stands there long enough for the tide to come in and lick it all away.)

They got into her car, wearing loose jackets made of nylon, shorts and jeans. She drove with the windows down, a Volkswagen with a good engine. The smell of heated tarmacadam and aching, new-cut grass came in as they drove. Small wooden bungalows all along the edge of the beach, couples and groups of children playing in the almost total darkness, their voices, squeals, cries. She had dabbed a little perfume behind her ears; in the mirror, she could see both of them cuddling up together, conspiring in giggles and occasional glances into the mirror, into her eyes. Why had she bothered? Her sister, she thought, was an ungrateful bitch and spoiled, oh, that was our mother's fault. I took responsibility for everything, even telling her about her periods, for Christ's sake. Run up and see your big sister, she'll tell you what to do, and go into the bathroom; I heard it all the way up the stairs. Our mother was timid, frightened; our father sorted *that* out. They couldn't leave each other, they had nowhere to go. Nowhere to hide but each other. Strange, hellish place, that. Each other. I was there once too, Mum. I'm glad you're dead and I'm glad he's dead and I'm glad I'm alone. Neither of you taught me a bloody thing.

Out of the night the village lights were like fireflies. The street was full of couples eating ice-cream, enjoying the tepid evening, and outside the pubs fat-bellied young men sat in shorts swamping pints of beer and lager and whistling at the girls who went by in flimsy clinging skirts, arms folded protectively across their breasts. O, I did that breast-arms-folded thing too, once, sure I did. So that a man going by *wouldn't* stare at them; but there was nothing, nothing in the world to compare with what I felt when I saw what *he* felt, saw it in his face, when I opened my blouse and took off my bra and smiled, just smiled. Girls, girls, he stared and stared. I conquered him. Then he conquered me. Then I owned him. Then he left me. The litany is as old as love. It repeats itself forever, a bell. Ding-dong, ding-dong, the ever-expectant lovers' song. And there's nothing anyone can do about it.

I was going to Louisville, Kentucky. I told myself I was and I was. He just didn't ask me, that was all; he had a wife, he did the decent thing in the end. He was a decent man. She turned into a car-park, slowed the engine, turned it off, rolled up the windows, got out, not caring if the others did or did not. There were times, even now, when too much thinking about it all was not good for her. They were out of the car and slamming the door. I'm dying for a nice cool pint of lager, gurgle-gurgle, down the hatch! I want peanuts, buy me a bag of roasted peanuts. She let them go in ahead of her, she wanted to make her entrance alone, with some sense of dignity. But as she swung open the door he came back to her, grinned, took her shoulder, almost pushed her forward into the lounge bar. Don't be shy, now, tonight might be your big night. I hate you, she said to him, but she made no sound. I wish you were dead. They made their way into the smoky, noisy, juke-boxy room, the air solid with smoke and sweat. They sat near the lavatories and every time the doors opened they were treated to smells of urine and disinfectant. They looked around, spent a great deal of their silent time staring into other people's faces. Her sister chewed peanuts and drank vodka. He sat there, gulping the golden pints and trying to bite her sister's shoulders. Once, a man on a bar-stool had looked in her direction and smiled, but she had tried to hold his stare and lost it. She knew when she looked at him that there was no question, she would have taken him back to the bungalow and to her bed. The other two would sleep on the floor beneath the table and the cockroaches would come in towards dawn. She drank glasses of beer and looked around her and saw the intense light emptiness of everything; laughter was the result of too much alcohol, the perfume, when it passed her, was cheap, the men were anxious and good-looking enough and too blatant. Her man on the bar-stool disappeared. Suddenly she felt tired, exhausted by everything and by nothing. Life exhausted her. What was the point in all of this, a weekend at the bungalow? She looked at his hands on her sister's neck and saw the dark hairs there and wondered, just for a precious instant, whether her sister loved him. This is all too tedious, too difficult, too foolish, too exasperating. Gleams of light through the beer glass; artificial, but beautiful. I'm getting drunk. The heat, the smoke, my throat with cigarette smoke. She went into the ladies to toss water on her face and found that the water-taps were screwed tight and the towel fell in folds all over the floor from the dispenser and whoever said women were tidier than men? In the toilet cubicle she read crude and stupid graffiti and wondered if one day, perhaps, she would turn into the kind of woman who scrawled such frustration on the walls of toilets. She stared at her face in a sink mirror and saw gentle wrinkles, big eyes, a decent mouth. That was all. It took more than that. To get a man to leave his wife in Louisville, Kentucky. It took more than all these things put together. But what it took exactly, she'd never been able to find out.

The little round table full of glasses and wet with slopped drink; the crowded smoky room, the artificial laughter, the tight feeling of being closed in by it all; she dreamed. He had searched the music shops for Giuseppe Allighiero who, he told her frantically, had composed a brilliant work for guitar, the Artemis Concerto, the year after Handel's death. Allighiero – he had trained his tongue to trot gracefully around the Italian's name – had been one of the first for whom the guitar, as opposed to the flute, had become a serious instrument. Like Handel – he had dragged himself closer to her across the grass, while the city sang around them and a cricket match tocked and lazed, white flannels, smell of leather and linseed oil, a hundred yards over the mown lawns – he had turned late in life to religious music. The Artemis Concerto was his last secular work, written painfully in a borrowed set of rooms in Florence – Allighiero had developed rheumatism, and was slowly sliding into insanity, there were rages, fits, as a result of syphilis – and you should hear it, you should hear it, it has all the heat, dust, stifling airless frenzy of the man in those days. It sounds uncomfortable, if a piece of music can be called that, she'd said. Thwock of leather ball on bat, a shout, another shout, and she had averted her eyes to their rolled-up white shirts and the billowing trousers which looked so good on them. No, no, he'd said, it was condensed into passion, pure energetic passion. Just like we have when we fuck, she'd said; and he'd noticed, then, the curious tick of bewilderment, the nervous shock of suddenly failing to recognise her. He leaned back on his knees and smiled. That's not how I'd put it, but OK Giuseppe Allighiero; he breathed the words, then, as if to reaffirm their holiness after her profanity. If I could get hold of the music of the Concerto, you'd hear something. I know a little of the first part; I'll try it when we get back. Fuck me first, then we'll get to Allighiero, she said. Too much watching the white flannels, sails filled with sex, the smell of the grass and the heat; she wanted him, wanted somebody, felt her dryness melt and moisten. Sitting there on the grass. Most wonderful open feeling, the nervous desire, the warmth in the belly; I want to see your face above me pucker and eyes grip, I want to hear you. I want to. She had reached out, had touched the inside of his thigh, he had enclosed her hand with his. Then, blatantly, brilliantly, he had moved down sinuously and covered her from toe to head, her legs opening, the light skirt riding up, his weight concentrated downwards between her thighs, push, release, push, release, drawing her upwards rhythmically as he released, letting her fall away as he pushed; his mouth swallowed her, her tongue darted forward like a fat wet frog and he sucked it, and she heard the shock of wood on leather again, thought of the whiteness, the bared arms, the sunlight on everything, and dissolved against his hardness. He let her breathe; we can't do it here, not here, no. They'd gone to the hired car and there, his trousers round his ankles, she'd squatted over him, absorbed him, driven him inside her and felt his fingernails nip the flesh of her back and buttocks. He'd called her name, grunted into her ear, then held her to him tightly, eagerly, with the same frantic thing that caught hold when he talked about Giuseppe Allighiero. Christ, you are the best thing that ever happened to me. I don't want to leave you. I don't want to. Christ, I don't want to. Then don't, she'd said, and listened to his breathing become regular, the pleading over.

Driving now against a fine mist of rain, drunk enough to be careful. In the rear mirror he gropes my sister, hand under the vest, the usual crappy obviousness, nothing about him in the least way lyrical. A crud. A walking death. Belly-and-fart. And the way he eyes me, as if I haven't known better. O yes. O yes, my son. I have. Beyond your reckoning. And I'm still in love, bitter love, with him, with that. We pulsed towards each other like metronomic certainties, timed to miniature perfections; when he withdrew from me, every time he did, I felt as if the earth had been pulled out of me, I was empty again. And I found it, the music. I found it, almost out of my mind with loneliness, anguish, the pain no one knows about because it's different every time. He was gone, it was the saddest day of my life, I put him on the airport bus, refused to go, no, I couldn't stand that, but it was bad enough, his eyes had tears in them, faces pressed to the windows, the movement of the bus too inevitable, too unbeatable, we couldn't do anything, and I kissed the glass and waited, waited for the bus to be out of sight before I collapsed onto a bench and wept. Fuck you fuck you, you don't know, you'll never know what that night was like, or the next morning. I knew death then and consequently cannot fear dying anymore. I knew for sure this time that God did not exist and that nothing ever saved us. We were ourselves and a few friends, and sometimes not even that much. I cried, screamed, banged my face with my fists, masturbated without strength, without lust because lust requires hope and I'd none of that commodity. Snot on my lips, wiped away on the back of my hand. I hated myself, hated the emptiness you'd left me. Time healed part of it; only part. Nothing like that is ever completely healed. I found the damned music. While I was still crazy enough, still believed he'd walk in any time, I found a tiny music shop in a back street and out came this tattery-edged copy, printed in the 1920s, of the Collected Concertos of G.A. Allighiero, the 'A' standing for Antonio, and there in the fusty pages was the Artemis Concerto; with a footnote. Allighiero's sister Faustina had been slighted in love, wounded, as they say, in her youth; a sour spinster, she had grown up despising, not all men, but all *women*, on the grounds that they still had their virginity to lose or, having lost it to men who still loved them, knew sexual bliss. Women became the token of her own unrequited love, virginity thrown away, as she saw it, for nothing, leaving her with only the memory, the after-taste, of one night of passionate indulgence. Her love had been so strong that it had translated with proportionate ease into revenge; revenge on her own sex for the promise of their lust. Her own she stubbornly refused to acknowledge and died in great poverty – her brother had little or no money – in a hovel. The lover is reputed to have been a friend of Allighiero, possibly another musician. He was never named. The composer had dedicated the concerto to his sister. Irony. Madness. Madness. A two-beat word which conveys little or nothing. Mist on the windows, the increasing tang of salt. Down here, the headlights breaking through the irregular dunes, sand blowing out of the ridges and crests. There, along the beach, squat blot of the bungalow. I refused to send it to him. I too had a moment's revenge. I don't know where it is now; I could find it if I really looked. There. In the mirror they grow embarrassed. Out. Cold night air, chill in the bones. He looks at me, eyes bleared by beer, she says: can we use your bed tonight? It's so bloody uncomfortable in sleeping-bags on the floor. You'll get used to it, I say obliquely.

There are worse places. They shuffle off, towards a joint of marijuana and a quickie before I get back. For I am going for a walk. Maybe tonight's my night to walk into the sea. No, leave that for another night, when there's nothing else. For there have been moments, I tell you. There have. Odour of salt, of ocean, of world's open wound, world's terminus. I close my jacket, button by button, assiduous little girl. I stroll against the wind, in the dark, with a moon full and unbearably white, risen high, gentling the sea with a silver landing-strip for angels. I went mad with him; went mad. Under the rain of a thousand nights, on the concrete of hundreds of streets, I wept for him. The letters drifted down like the last flakes in a snowstorm. Then even their light went out. You don't know. The sea on my right hand, the earth on my left, on I walk, unable to fly. And I think, now, of Faustina Allighiero, of the depth of pain; of the need, almost, for its renewal. I come here at weekends and try to ease myself back into myself, into the skin of the old salamander that was me. But I do not change. He has moulded me in the image of something stricken and made foolish; is that how I appear to the world? A foolish woman? Nothing more than that? Sea to my right, earth to my left, and there, there under the warmth of the moon a unicorn, lightly on the footpath of moonlight coming nearer.

(Where'd your mad sister go? he asked her, snug in the folds of the sleeping-bag; the tang of his semen came up to him when he shifted his legs. She lay a few inches from him, wrapped tightly, cocooned. He stubbed out the joint on the rough floorboards; fuck you, this is all too weird, he said. What's too weird? she said; and why are you angry at me? Where's your sister gone? It's dark out there. Why should you worry, you don't like her. I never said that, when did I ever say that? You think she's mad, her silences, the way she looks at you. No, he said, he had never thought she was mad. And he hadn't noticed the way she looked at him. Raising herself up on her elbow, her face coming up from the sleeping-bag; you just said she was mad. Anyway, I have the feeling that you'd like to screw her all the same, mad and all as you think she is. He is silent. He wants to get out of the bag and look for her, he is afraid, but he cannot convey this fear to anyone. It is not permitted to be afraid, you must never fear anything. Yes I would screw her, if that's what it comes down to, he thinks; but what he says is: She's too old, for Christ's sake. But she definitely needs a man. She had one, she says; and then there is silence, and he is afraid, sitting propped up on both elbows staring into the ragged shapes of darkness in the room, feeling the approach of cockroaches, hearing the distant sea, seeing through one pane of window-glass the moon, a single threatening point of round light. O God, why am I so afraid?)

Orangeman

He sat up at the table. His aunt hurried in with a plateful of pota-
to chips and eggs. She leaned over him, a thin-armed woman
always in a rush, and she raised the volume of the radio for the
BBC news. As far as he could tell she always listened to the news
and at the same time every day. She almost ran back into the
kitchen. Through the door he could see her ironing the white
silk gloves, back and forth, with great care, leaning on the iron.

His father fluttered a newspaper. He was standing by the
fireplace. Eat that quick, his father said; don't keep Ernie waiting. He crammed chips and portions of egg into his mouth
until he could barely move his jaw. Upstairs his cousin Sarah
knocked something over. He glanced up at the ceiling. Don't
you delay, his father said.

Are you sure you'll not have a wee cup of tea? his aunt called
to his father.

No thanks, Harriet. I'm all right.

A wee cup in your hand as you're standing there? No, I'm
fine, thanks Harriet. You'll be glad of it later, his aunt said,

dashing in with a cup on a saucer. A wee sandwich, in your hand? Aye. Just one. Okay.

His father threw the newspaper onto the couch. The white cat gave a little leap and disappeared under an armchair, leaving long wiry white hairs on the cushion. The chips were big fat ones, and he speared them now and mopped up the egg yolk with a circular movement on the plate. He wiped his chin. His aunt scampered in with a mug of tea.

Did that do you? Did you like that all right? Aye, he said. Thanks very much

Say 'Thanks Very Much Aunt Harriet' his father said from the couch.

Thanks very much, Aunt Harriet.

Och sure there's no time for formalities the day, his aunt said with a quick laugh. He sat up at the table and drank his tea and caught scraps of news from the radio.

Uncle Ernie called out from the front room – a deep, solid shout. His aunt picked up the gloves by their cuffs, carefully, watching them. She carried them through to the front room with infinite care. When she passed through again she wiped her hands against the sides of her legs.

Are youse all right in here? Youse have enough of everything? Oh, I've forgotten that sandwich.

Don't worry about it, his father said; but she came back with a sandwich. That man inside drives me crazy every year with his gloves and hat and shoes and socks, she said to no one in particular, retreating back into the kitchen. She began searching for a clothes brush, found one, charged through the room again. When she returned she carried the sash over one arm, the tassels fluttering wildly in her airstream.

He turned in his chair and looked at his father. He was going bald. His fingers tapped idly on the edges of the white china cup. Crumbs scattered round the edges of his mouth.

You've got crumbs on you.

Thanks, his father said, and he wiped his mouth with the back of his hand. He looked at his father. Are we going up to the hospital the night? Mmm-mmm, his father said. Later, later. He stood up from the table. Do you want more tea?

There's plenty in the pot, his aunt called from the kitchen. It's just I can't pour it with the wee jobs this man has me doing.

I'm all right, his father said. We should be pushing off soon.

His aunt charged through with the ironed sash. He drained the mug. His father stood up, took his mug, moved off into the kitchen. Upstairs his cousin Sarah dropped something. He stepped out into the hallway just as his Uncle Ernie came out of the parlour.

The golden sash crossed his uncle's black suit in a V-shape, shining almost against the dark cloth. His aunt busily pinned the last of the glinting silver decorations, then the capital letters 'L.O.L.' onto the front of the sash. His uncle, huge and broadly outlined against the hallway, carefully adjusted his spotless gloves. His aunt fussed and nipped invisible buds of dust from the black bowler hat. The trousers, black and sharply creased, rested their upturned ends on the broad shiny black leather of the shoes. The tie wore a silver Lodge-pin. I think I'll just about do, said his uncle. The round red face, which always reminded him of drawings of childhood elves, puckered into a craggy smile. Ruts and creases and crevasses appeared over it.

He giggled back at his uncle, not at anything he'd said, but at the appearance of the wrinkled face. His uncle took wide, awkward steps in front of the hall mirror. Get your Da out here, son, it's time we were away.

I can't wait for you, his uncle shouted suddenly up the stairs. Make your own way over, Sarah.

Sarah, long-legged, dark-haired, bounded down the stairs. He looked at his cousin, recognising something worth looking at in her, though he wasn't sure what it was. Are you right, Da? he shouted and his father came into the hallway.

Enjoy yourselves, his aunt said. She opened the door and they shuffled out, his father leading, to the car. Down the street a door opened. A man dressed in bowler hat and sash, carrying a raincoat over his arm, emerged. His uncle waved. Got your marching-boots on you the day, Jimmy?

They got into the car. He sat beside his cousin Sarah and when she moved her leg against his he felt uncomfortable. Right, his uncle said; you know where to drop me off. His father drove out of the street, turned into the main road, drove quickly towards town. Along the pavements groups of men walked hurriedly, all dressed in black suits, bowler hats, sashes. They laughed and scampered across streets – young, old, out-for-the-day, out for the laugh. He looked out at them and then at his uncle's huge, red, pitted neck, rising out of the tight white collar. He remembered Father Martin, his hands clasped behind his back, instructing his class to find alternative routes into the centre of the city past Carlisle Circus; there had been an Orange parade, some stone-throwing, the army had been called out. Father Martin said it was a case of provocation. He could not imagine a man such as his Uncle Ernie marching arrogantly, wilfully, into a Catholic area simply to provoke trouble. He heard his uncle's thick, open-hearted laugh. He felt that odd mixture of embarrassment and excitement that seemed to accompany this day. He felt part of all of this and not part of it at the same time; divided, unsure of himself, a foot on either side of an almighty stroke of history and place. And he felt the need to explain himself, but to whom or what he could never say.

Not long after the war his father had met a woman from Dublin who worked in a big city-centre shop and married her. Dapper, elegant, hair oiled and parted (he'd seen the photographs), his father had taken religious instruction and become a Roman Catholic in order to do so.

When his father's mother died, it was Uncle Ernie who telegrammed. Had the little wounds healed? His grandfather had fended for himself in his last years, a big, wheezing, stubborn figure, quietly tolerant. Once he had spread all his war medals out on the lino-covered table and pointed to them without saying anything. A sad old man, stranded, in a way. He had died of pneumonia and old age. The house had been sold.

They approached the Orange Hall. Men in black suits crowded around outside. This is fine, Uncle Ernie said. I'll see you all back at the house later. We might go up to the hospital, his father said. Sarah got out, and he relaxed. He looked through the window and saw her running to a young man on a motorbike. A quaint turning-over in his stomach; the motorcycle drove off, the wind whipping up Sarah's skirt. If you go to the hospital, drop in on the way home then and let me know how she is.

His uncle moved up the steps ponderously, staggering a little. Men reached out their hands, slapped him on the back. Happy-faced men, out for a good time. Were these men dangerous?

He remembered as they drove away from the hall the twinge of shame he had felt in Creavy's English History class when big bull-faced Creavy, reading out a passage referring to an uprising some time during the 1800s in which several Protestant farmers had been killed, had commented viciously: they should *all* have been driven out, the whole bloody lot of them. And McClure, standing up at the back of the class, had cheered and thrust his fist into the air. The shame had cut him through like a knife. Sir, he had said, cautiously, feeling his way; that's not fair, is it, sir? What's not fair about it, boy?

At that moment he had acknowledged fear. For the first time in his life, on the point of defending Protestantism, he had been in hostile territory, without supporters. Across the city from the college, where he lived and played each day amongst Protestants, he would have found a sympathy he now realised he could not hope to arouse here, in his own classroom. The feeling was very odd, ironic, almost amusing. What's not fair? Creavy asked him again. He wanted to answer for his uncles, his aunts, Sarah, his father also; but he could not open his mouth. Stupidly, he excused himself and sat down, full of shame. Don't give *me* a history lesson, boy, Creavy said, and moved on to something else. He had felt McClure's eyes needling into him – the curious, almost embarrassed glances from the others in the class. A suspicion thrown his way. He felt relieved, he had to admit, when nothing came of it afterwards.

He leaned back in the seat. They drove behind the City Hall. I'm going to park somewhere, his father said; we can watch from Royal Avenue. His father parked the car. Soldiers strolled carelessly in the grounds of the City Hall. The footpaths were cordoned off from the roadway. Already, as they walked briskly around the City Hall grounds and approached Royal Avenue, the sounds of solid, drumping-drumping drums and screeching whistles carried over the centre of the city. They lifted the cordon-ropes and scampered across the empty street, lifting another rope and diving into the tight, pressing crowd in Royal Avenue. The sun shone steadily on the green dome of the City Hall; starlings exploded from the thin-limbed trees, breaking in flocks over Robinson and Cleaver's, the window-shades pulled down, bearing the legend 'Tailors to His Majesty The King'. An army helicopter puttered in the distant blue sky, like a tiny annoying insect, circling tightly over and over the centre of the city. What could they see from up there but the waiting, cordoned streets, the black spread of people on the pavements; and somewhere the steadily advancing first bands, the banners heaving, the white-shirted players tramping noiselessly a thousand feet below?

In the crowd there was very little air and it was hot. He removed his pullover. Everyone looked down the wide avenue but there was nothing to see. Still the sounds grew louder, more distinct. Drums tack-tack-tacking, thrumping monotonously, the scream of whistles, the rhythm of a march. And almost impossible to hear, yet lilting strangely above the rest, the steady cat's yelp of bagpipes. His father blew smoke across the cordon; he watched it flutter and disperse against the white roadway. Glancing up to the rooftops he saw two or three soldiers take up squatting positions; one soldier adjusted a radio on his back. If someone opened fire in this crowd, he wondered, how would anyone survive? He strained his neck out over the rope and looked down the avenue. Something seemed to shiver in the crowd. I can see nothing, someone said. But they're on the way.

The whistles were silent. A sudden rhythmic explosion of drums – hard, like bullets splattering against a steel door; then again, a pause, and once more. Keeping the marching in step. Louder now. The persistent chattering of starlings along the eaves of the buildings around him drowned in a wave of flute music as the march tunes started up again. *Derry's Walls; Lilliburlero*. And the crowd rippled and shifted like wavelets on a pond disturbed by an abrupt breeze. He arched his neck out over the cordon-rope and immediately he saw the first band, the banners blue and red and gold, flapping and crackling in the breeze, the thick white guy-ropes, heavy in the hands of the wee lads, short-trousered, giddy-faced, trotting to keep up with the march. The players were stripped to immaculate, blinding-white shirts, swaying slightly from the hips upwards, their music-stands projecting from the thick black flutes; the drummers hammered the rhythm-beats out with each upwards swing of the knee, the snow-white lanyards dangling below the drums in time with the steps. And in front of the players a young man raced backwards and forwards, flinging a long, silver-headed baton high into the air, not breaking the sway of his step as he looked up quickly, noted its loop and fall, and retrieved it expertly as it came down, tossing it round behind his back, heaving it up in the opposite hand and launching it once more into the air. The banner bore the image of a tall man in white gaiters against a background of sailing-ships and the motto Faith, Unity, Strength: L.O.L. 798, Siddons Memorial; Ravenhill Road. And behind the white-shirt-ed band strode the members of the Lodge, black-suited, bowler-hatted, proud, aloof, every face steadily forward. He could feel their pride; he always did. Every year it was the same: the sound of the bands; the solemn, prideful, marching men; the snap and applause of the banners. A rush of defiance spread over him and something like hunger awoke in his belly. How could he explain to anyone why he wanted to march out there too, to be part of it, to be not one least bit removed from his Uncle Ernie and the rest of the striding, white-gloved men who filed in front of him now, oblivious to the soldiers on the rooftops, the helicopter fluttering overhead, the arrogant starlings – to everything but their own importance and sense of belonging. Could there be any doubt that these men owned the ground they marched over? Could there be any doubting their faith in themselves, their defiance of intrusion? If he had Creavy here now, or McClure, he would shove him up to the cordon-rope, *force* him to look, *force* him to say something derogatory in the face of such disciplined faith and order. He realised he was clapping his hands vigorously. Stop clapping, his father said.

The Glasgow bands: some people said they caused trouble on the boat on the way over. A white-shirted, blue-trousered band slashing out *Dolly's Brae*, crashing the great blast of drums and fifes and whistles from one side of the street to the other, the enormous bass drum thundering out a solid persistent beat, the banner proclaiming St Andrew's Road, Glasgow, L.O.L. 51; In God we Serve. Behind them a wee ludicrous fat man almost rolled over beneath a Lambeg drum, beating the rattan canes against the sides of the drum with a clatter like stones belting off a corrugated tin roof; but in time, menacingly, the war-drum still fearsome and disturbing in the wide street. He tried to fix his eyes on the wee man's knuckles to see if they bled. The bagpipers followed, ahead of two crawling black limousines. The screaming pipes completely obliterated the patient sound of the car engines. Elderly men waved slowly from the windows – men too old to march, honoured, driven to the Field. An enormous banner, gold-tasselled, blue-clothed, straining against the breeze like the billowing sail of a ship; the image of a man in red robes leaning on a short pillar with a bible in his hand; long white curling hair, down to his shoulders; L.O.L. 138; Macklin Road and District; Reverend Samuel Frazier: 1799–1848; I Place My Trust In Thee. And he saw his Uncle Ernie, the white gloves flashing to and fro, sharp white streaks of light against the dark trousers. He waved and shouted but his Uncle Ernie did not turn his head. He stared into his uncle's face as he strode past him, carried away, it seemed, in the flood of black-clad, sashed marchers around him. But his pride was a solid knot in his belly. It did not let him go.

Kilts, white shirts, banners breaking in the breeze; a steady, incredible, endless tramping up Royal Avenue, turning at the City Hall, going and coming as if forever; a shattered drum. He stared at it all, transfixed by the noise, the colour, the pride. There was nothing else in his experience to compare with what he saw each year. This flesh-and-blood, drum-and-fife embodiment of tradition and faith overpowered him. It left him with an inner emptiness, a little void he could not fill with anything else. Why did he also feel, obscurely, a vague bitterness? Father Martin, staring down the college avenue from the steps, seeing his parents and himself into the car; college sports day. A convert, Mr Thomson. I'm very glad to hear that. You must be very proud, Mrs Thomson. Conversion usually makes for stronger faith. His father, bending in to the car; he could feel his father's embarrassment. In himself he felt the first motions of a troubled anger. His mother, smiling-proud of what she had made his father do in order to marry her. What had it really been like, all those years ago? How had his father felt, hearing the door of his family home slam shut, to be opened only gradually, on the sly, as the years passed? All for the sake of this woman who prided herself now and then that somebody recognised her in the street from the war years, and called her by the nickname they'd used in those ancient days, Rosie, for her bright red hair. Father Martin waving a discreet hand as his father turned the car down the avenue and onto the main road. Silence all the way home. Earlier she had made a fool of herself. Martin had been ill in his youth; he mentioned it, over tea. Oh, Frank was in Purdysburn, Father, his mother had said; he had watched his father wince, curl up, withdraw. The Fever Hospital, Father, she added. Ah, yes, the priest said, relaxing. Ha-ha. In the car, all the way home, silence. An embarrassing woman. He had left his religion and his family to marry her. Now that she was dying, what did he know of his father's thoughts?

They drove through dark, uneasy streets to the hospital. The army used part of it. They had to drive through a checkpoint; his father showed a pass through the windows. It began to rain. Soft, slight rain, drifting down over the great black shadow of Divis. The car slipped to a stop. His father rubbed his eyes. The squat outlines of armoured ambulances huddled against a wall, their huge red crosses jumping out from the riveted rear doors. His father was used to the hospital, he knew where to go. They moved along a thin empty corridor, then up a flight of stairs. His father spoke in a whisper to a doctor and a nurse. The entire floor was silent, nothing moved anywhere, and his father's urgent whisperings seemed too loud. The doctor and the nurse withdrew. He heard their footsteps on the stairs.

The little room was heavy with a sickly rotting smell which seemed to invade everywhere. He had never known anything like it – a sweet, sharp odour of decay. She lay with her mouth open, her face yellow, snoring lightly; the hideously enlarged left arm rested awkwardly on top of the bedclothes. She was almost entirely bald now. They had provided a red wig; her thick red hair had been a source of great pride to her. His father called her name a couple of times but her mouth did not move, her head remained sunken into the thick pillow. He fidgeted, unable to feel anything for this woman who would very soon be dead. His father was confused, he stood looking at her, walked around the bed, looked again. He produced a single bottle of stout, placed it on the bedside table. They stepped into the hall. She's on the way out, his father said. But he could feel nothing. The woman was a stranger. What had she been like years and years ago, when he must have argued with his own father about her, prepared to change his entire life for her? What did his father feel on a day such as this, watching that great loud celebrating of endurance and strength coursing the main streets of the city, proud and defiant under the sun; unable forever to participate? And this woman who had caused his separation from it, her fading breathing, encased in an odour of decay and death, still confusing him.

We'll call in on Ernie, his father said outside in the rain. An armoured ambulance shivered and its engines started. It revved and barked and backed out and drove off towards the city. His father switched on the windscreen wipers.

A dirty oul' night, said his father, and they drove away from the hospital.

Speaking English

These days I remember Patel.

I remember the afternoon I helped him look for a flat. A dull afternoon, burdened with city rain, he kept complaining about his turban. It felt twice as heavy, he explained, laden with water. Now and then we would stop in a doorway and he'd straight- ˙t. Every room shone with the dull light of winter. I was out work and spent too much time reading newspapers in the pub, glancing over the top of the page to see who'd come in, who'd know me and buy me a drink. Being out of work had dropped me farther inside myself than I'd ever have imagined possible. There were other people, real people, and there was me. In the evenings the anonymity of the pub suited me and I could relax. Sometimes there was music, my few drinking bud- dies, and lost souls like Patel who wandered in out of some per- sonal cold and tried to get accepted and find a place to be. Patel joined us that winter all the way from Calcutta. It seemed, to most of us, an unfair swap. He was a medical student and he sipped orange juice with cubes of ice in it and smiled a lot. His

English was good. In truth, not even *he* knew why he was with us.

He was trying hard to grow a moustache. I noticed this as we sat down on the top of the bus, how vague the moustache was. When I remarked it that day he smiled and told me it was one of his ambitions, to have a moustache. I had one. We were young. We saw the world in simple terms.

And I remember the colour of those stone steps and walking up, and the interminable rain down my back, my hair matted to my skull. The black-iron railings, the spear-heads, the smell of dogs and the smoke from chimneys, rising so straight into the metal sky it might have been sucked up by straws. The windows of these houses seemed to protest at the audacity of our advance. We looked at each other, and Patel lifted the heavy black door-knocker. A thin, pleasant-faced woman in her late middle years opened the door; she gave off a faint whiff of iodine. Patel smiled and reminded her that she had advertised a room. She seemed to have forgotten, she looked from Patel to me and from me back to Patel. She remembered, then, that the room was gone, and she was very sorry. Patel smiled and, as I recall, bowed slightly. We went down the steps into the rain again. Over a cup of coffee I apologised to Patel. For what? he said, his hands out in front of him, palms upward. That damning smile. Some of my fellow-students have been looking for a place for months, Patel said; they remain quite unenlightened by their experiences. They still believe that in Ireland no one will reject them because of the colour of their skin.

It was a café with a loud juke-box and Patel had to shout. We became friends out of this indignity, in the loose fashion of the times. Patel found a claustrophobic bedsit in a tenement of bedsits; we crowded in to celebrate. Four of us, three on the bed, the host on the floor against a single window, and the sound of rock music from other places in the building and the odour of frying, spices, and the crackle of Asian voices. Patel found acceptance in this miniature ghetto. He was where he was expected to be. Other places were for other people, he had learned that. We argued, got drunk, sang. There is no discrimination, most of the time, among the outer classes.

Now that was a long time ago and I was driving my son Paul to the airport. He will be ten this Christmas. He spends his summers with me and the rest of the time with his mother, an amicable and civilised arrangement. His mother was once my beautiful wife, my Flower of the Nile. I spent a year expanding my horizons – what a phrase! – just after the *affaire Patel*. I was teaching English in a small, hot secondary school just outside Cairo. One day I went for a trip to the pyramids and fell. My wife was a nurse in the clinic where they patched me up. I called back and kept calling. Her name was Jennifer. She told me she had an Arabic name that would be too difficult to pronounce. She was tall, slim, eyes like burnt almonds, shy. She hadn't travelled much, liked Egypt, wanted to take further exams. For the moment, life in the clinic among the old women with painted faces and henna on their hands was sufficient. Her mother had given her the name Jennifer, a name redolent of cucumber sandwiches and cold beer, as a token of the esteem in which she held the British for whom she had scrubbed floors during the Second World War. I told her I'd had an uncle who'd served in the Air Force in Cairo in that war and he'd lost three fingers through frostbite. The desert is a cold place, said Jennifer enigmatically. I fell in love with her. Her father looked me over once, a beaming man with grey crinkling hair, opened his immaculately white shirt and welcomed me. Her family were Christian, though no more fanatical about the business than I was. She had a sister, another nurse, in New York and a brother in military service. In the evenings we walked along dusty roads to the echo of the *muezzin* calling the Muslim faithful to prayer, while all around us clanked pushbikes, piloted with careless determination by what appeared to be great billows of white cotton. The sun went down with a soft plop, like a dark orange dropped in a basin. We sat in tiny withered parks and listened to the chatter of old men with walking sticks and faded suits and brilliant, aristocratic moustaches. Black tobacco scented the alleyways where we visited Jennifer's relatives, doors splashing great daubs of Van Gogh yellow on the sand as they opened, mint tea, cakes, hands that flew like birds from table to cutlery, children with big black eyes who stared at me. I did not want to leave, I did not want to go anywhere, I had found my world. We married, a quiet ceremony with a reception that seemed to last for days; Jennifer's father, a small official in the local council, had seen to everything. A small army of friends and family smothered the house. I wrote home and told my parents their only child was now a married man.

I took my wife home with me. My mother, hanging back in the kitchen like a wounded animal hiding in a thicket, rubbed her hands. Jennifer was visibly nervous. My father offered her the last of the Christmas whiskey; she refused. After a time, when we'd eaten and endured the first of many silences around the kitchen table, my mother managed to work my wife out of the room. My father was frank. She's gorgeous, son. What you mean is, Dad, you think I've let myself in for problems.

Seeing one's father embarrassed is itself acutely embarrassing. He is, as one's father, supposed to know everything. Suddenly it is revealed that he does not. Everyone is let down. It hurt. He offered me a cigarette. We smoked, got pally. You're both very young, my father said. And people in this country can be very bloody odd. He didn't seem to be enjoying his cigarette. Above my father's head, framed, on the wall, a very old portrait of Pope John XXIII. My father sighed. If there are ever any problems, you just let me know. It was his way of admitting utter defeat. I don't envisage any problems, Dad, I said. He looked at me as if he'd never seen me before. None so intolerant, you know, as those who have once been colonised, he said. I was impatient to leave, to confront the world outside without my father's strangled offers of help. I began to see my parents as a waste of time, a cynical and damning view and ultimately unfair. But, after all, my life – with all its needs, terrors, dreads, assortment of anxieties – had been a procession of carefully-rehearsed escapes from them. My mother came back into the room, pushing my wife gently before her. I knew from my mother's smile and Jennifer's hardened stare at me that lines had been drawn across which Jennifer would not be permitted to step. Of course, Mam, I should have married *one of our own*, as they say. That would have made you happy. When I said goodbye to my parents that day we were no longer friends. I wanted to leave them forever. And I was suddenly afraid of them. The fatal alchemy of love and fear.

My wife decided to resume her studies. One day she came back and told me how all the Asian and African students seemed to huddle together; she understood why, she said, she had tried mixing but had felt an uncomfortable itch just to the right of her heart, a sure sign, she explained, that somewhere or other, somehow or other, she was being patronised. Anyway, the huddling Asians and Africans disturbed her and the white students, most likely not meaning to, made her feel that she had been taken aboard as a passenger. With almost frightened, at least bewildered eyes, my wife said, the black students stared around the enormous canteen between lectures, as if waiting for a signal or a secret sign that all was not quite well with the world, it was time to go. She sat on my lap to tell me this, and I played with my hair. Later, as we lay in bed, I told her the one about how, as schoolchildren, we'd all been made to give a penny or two for the support of the little black children, children – we were assured – just like us, who were not having as good a time as we were having and who were far, far away. My wife stared at the ceiling; she hadn't heard this one. That's wonderful, my wife said; now that we're all here, what are you going to do with us? I was just about to say that she hadn't lived the life of the children for whom we'd donated our pennies, that she'd been well off. I know what you're thinking, my wife said in the darkness; your intentions are good. Look at my mother, who adores the people for whom she scrubbed floors, what can you do with a woman like that? But I tell you, dear husband, I would not particularly feel that I owed you my love simply because, thousands of miles away when we were both children, you gave up your pocket-money to avoid being frowned at by your schoolteacher.

And my wife patted my privates twice with her open hand and fell asleep.

Summer arrived. My wife looked stunning. We walked through the city like royalty, she wore a particularly attractive shy look. We ate ice-cream and then sat at a wrought-iron table outside a delicatessen and sipped tea while she wrote a letter home. There were the city smells of diesel and coffee percolating. I read in a morning newspaper about rioting in a place called Soweto. I took my eyes off the print and put them on the lowered face of my wife, scribble scribble, a fine neat hand in ballpoint on blue airmail paper, long eye-lashes, black tidy hair. Her skin seemed to throb in the sunlight. Suddenly I was terrified of losing her. She looked up and I was staring at her; she said later that my mouth was open. She smiled back. I knew I could lose her. Every man has a moment of that. When he realises, without wanting to, that nothing is forever. Well, I went back to the comparative distance of the riots in Soweto. How, I wondered, would we have fared in South Africa, where just being alone in the same room with her meant trouble with the law? Would we fight the world for each other? I drew myself away from the page, the headlines, and looked over that wide two-laned street with the potted plants on the island in the middle. Trees hummed over our heads and the big buses cruised past like enormous metal insects. Were we in a happy land, she and I? Had we come to Paradise? What if this were Soweto, and I courting her in secret, afraid, thief-like, guilty about feeling guilty? We had it easy, I thought. Even people like Patel. For some there was always a way out. And I felt a curious treacherous tingle of contempt for my wife; where a moment before I had felt something akin to horror at the prospect of losing her.

That evening she told me she was pregnant. Mixed emotions, probably common enough. I rang my parents, I was half-drunk by this time. I looked out from the 'phone-kiosk in the bar and winked hideously at Jennifer, who sat sedately with her hands in her lap, a coke on the table in front of her. Instead of telling my father, who was first to the 'phone as usual, about Jennifer's pregnancy, I came out with a curiously frantic burst of seemingly unrelated material. They're lovely people, I said. Who? asked my father. Lovely people, I said; Jennifer's parents. Oh, my father said. Not like you two, I told him. Look, son, I don't really know what this is all about, my father said, and I cut him down, cut them both down. Not like you two, bigots, typical Paddy bigots with the full force of the once-downtrodden. No quarter, that's you. What the hell are you talking about, boy? my father said. He always addressed me as *boy* when he was angry and wanted to remind me that he was my father and there were limits for our intimacies. Bigots, I said, out of control by now. And Jennifer's mother is an angel and I have a hypocrite for a mother; I thank God they'll probably never meet you, the two of you. My father hung up. I stared stupidly into the mouthpiece for a moment or two. I went back to the table. Well? asked my gorgeous Jennifer. Promise me you'll never leave me, I said to her, standing up. What? Jennifer said, screwing up her face. I've put my head on the block, Jennifer. Sit down, please, my wife said. What are you saying to me? I sat down, groped for my drink. My parents are delighted, I said. I am glad. Yes, delighted. You know what parents are like, always wanting grandchildren.

My wife believed me. I'd been a fool, but the anger, the rage had come from somewhere. I vaguely suspected it had its source within myself.

A horrible thought. Besides, I was a literal, man-of-the-world educated type, different from my parents in all the best possible ways. Head on the block, Jennifer. Jennifer was so happy I wanted to scream.

Paul was born. Plump dark-eyed Paul. Jennifer breast-fed him and sent photographs of her new son back to Cairo with an easy regularity. From time to time I worked as a part-time teacher, standing in here and there for people who had discovered better things to do. Money was scarce, but we got a 'phone.

One evening I caught Jennifer trying to put a call through to Cairo. I scolded her; that's not the right word. I objected strongly, waving my arms about. I raised my voice, I don't know why. I was scared even with Paul. I was scared of the size of the hole she'd leave in my life if she went away. And I had a nagging feeling, all the time now, that things were not as tied down as they might have been. I couldn't say why. Jennifer had acquired friends, friends other than those I'd introduced her to, and I felt I was being usurped in some way, that my influence was being drained. Absurd, maybe. Certainly immature, feeling like that. But I was becoming increasingly unsure about, well, everything. Her friends were African or Asian, and they went out to films and cooked meals for one another and generally, to me, acted like a commune of some sort. I was beginning to see conspiracies everywhere. Jennifer was happy, these days. I took care of Paul when I had time and she went back to her studies and her friends once or twice a week and came home and told me all about what Aisha had said, and Malek, and Sam, who was from Singapore and whom I thought I'd met once, and I'd teach here and there and one evening it all got too much for me; me, the liberal. I went upstairs. Paul was asleep, his little body folded into itself like a shell. His dark-light skin seemed to stain the creased whiteness of the sheets. I crouched over and kissed him lightly on the head and he protested, muttering, without opening his eyes. I closed the door of the flat as if I were about to commit some terrible crime as soon as the lock clicked. I was leaving Paul, who was about two years old at this time, alone in the flat while I searched the town for his mother, my wife, and I could explain none of it to myself. I didn't have a car then, I took a bus into town, agonising at the bus-stop, on the bus wondering if my son would smother to death while I was on this outrageous mission. I was ashamed of myself, hurt by my own action and most of all by the thinking that had given rise to it. I was afraid that Aisha or Malek or Sam or someone else, someone with whom she had more in common because they were also in a kind of exile, would persuade her to go home, leave me, that this was not the place for her. I imagined all sorts of conversations, as the bus ploughed across the city. I found Jennifer in a back room of a bar near the university, where I thought she'd be. When she saw me she jumped up, rushed over, scared stiff that I'd brought bad news about Paul, I suppose. What are you doing here? was the next question. I had no answer for that. Come home, I said. She looked at me, those oval, wonderful eyes, no longer shy. She'd done something to her hair, tied it to one side, and there was the slightest hint of perfume. I felt defeated. Was there a life here I knew nothing about? A tiny, willowy, dark-haired girl with a heart-breaking smile introduced herself as Aisha. She stood beside us, touched my wife lightly on the arm. Is there something wrong? You look disturbed. I wanted to tell her to go away. I felt my own embarrassment rise like a wave of poison, choking me. I tried to smile. My wife, the woman I loved, stared at me with the kind of look one reserves for an enemy. Who is looking after Paul? Who have you got to look after my son? Of course, I might have guessed, Paul and Jennifer were in this together. They'd made me an outcast. It was ridiculous, but very real. Come home, Jennifer. Why? Am I doing something wrong? Who is minding Paul? Answer me! Jennifer was plucking my arm, Aisha was grinning, and behind them at the table, one or two others grinned also. Friendliness, I couldn't handle that. It threatened me. I'd sat amongst those faces in a different setting and then things were different all round. Then I was respected. Here, I was just causing a scene. I was having the kind of thoughts I would never have considered possible in a man like me. I'd marched, signed petitions, demonstrated, put my name on embassy registers; for God's sake, I'd even gone out to Africa to *teach*. I was the product of the liberal Sixties. And in this pub I hated them, the open faces, the friendliness, the tolerance. They didn't know me, these people. I'd never known them. Patel? Patel was a *cause*, Jennifer was my *wife*. Standing in that pub in front of her I saw with horror that I was a diluted version of my parents and little more. There were

things in life with which it was alright to experiment, liberalism being one of them; but when push came to shove, one's
prejudices tightened ranks. I wanted to yell at the faces around
the table, I wanted to shove the girl Aisha out of the way, shout
the kind of things that had turned my stomach when I was a
fiery student in line with the most militant protesters. Prick the
skin, and just below the surface lay this other animal, this terrified bigot. I wanted to cry, to beat my head with my fists, to
beat someone else's head; I was rooted to the floor by thongs of
hatred and shame. Jennifer was frantic by now, and there was
the sound, somewhere in the distance, of a siren, which seemed
to increase her anger. What have you done? You have left Paul
all alone? How? How could you do this? What do you think I
am doing that you follow me around? Do you think I am
deceiving you? Do you think that? What do you want me to do?
These are my friends. Look! There is nothing for you to fear.
And all smiles had diminished. Maybe this was the kind of thing
they'd come to expect. Maybe, too, they knew the reasons. At
any rate no one showed any sympathy for me, the man who, in
his jealousy, abandoned his child. In the street of course, Jennifer had hailed a taxi and left me to die. When I got back home
she was sitting reading by a two-bar electric fire. She looked up,
looked down. There was a healing calmness in the room which
I took advantage of. I slunk into the kitchen, made a cup of coffee, all the time afraid that even the clink of my spoon against
the side of the cup would break the peace. I hated myself. My
fear, what I'd felt in the pub, it all left a rotting-vegetable taste in
my mouth. My whole being was soured, in revolt. Had I, all my
life, kept my terrors at a distance, my prejudices in check, a mixture of assumed liberalism and self-righteousness? What was I,
if this were so, but an inflated balloon, which any amount of
direct conflict could burst?

My parents came over occasionally; my mother would sniff
the air of our rooms as if doom might be scented there. No
one ever said much. Safer topics, such as environmental pol-
lution, the fate of the whale, were discussed. Through it all,

my beautiful wife would nod and accept their views with an admirable condescension which neither of them noticed. She had gradually risen above them, I had not. I had been struck by the fact that I resembled them closely. I saw the world, whether I liked it or not, through the same cautious eyes. I used the same kind of terror of new things and suspicion of strangers to filter my relationships; but, until recently, I had refused to accept this. Did being Irish mean being constantly on the alert? Paul grew, round-faced, black-eyed, a luxurious soft tan, like melting butterscotch. He listened to everything, but I'll never know just how much he actually heard. His eyes would flit like big black beetles from one of my parents to the other; as if, seated at the table chewing their way through a few hours of our lives, they had come to present a sort of sideshow for his benefit and he wanted to take it all in. My mother would pat him on the head as they left, always on the point of saying something, but the words were too big for her mouth. One afternoon the same ritual of head-patting at the door was interrupted by my wife. He speaks English, she smiled, all her magnificent teeth showing. My mother was devastated and fled down the steps to the comparative safety of the city. My father adopted a military air, stiffened, shook Jennifer's hand and gave Paul a pound-note. Without saluting, he descended the steps after his wife, much as an officer might follow his men over the top of a trench, and with the same awkward-footed dignity.

I decided to seek out Patel and invite him for dinner. I was anxious to show my wife that I did not mean her to be shut away from people. By now she shunned the company of Aisha and the rest; chiefly, I guess because she feared a repeat performance of what I'd managed in the pub that night. She grew rather furtive in my presence and I suspected she'd spoken to Cairo somehow. She dared not use the 'phone for this purpose when I was in the flat. I hated myself intensely for Jennifer's discomfort. But I was quite powerless to do anything about it by now. Anything to do with Africa threatened me. I would hold myself in with a great effort during the television news; when anything about Africa *did* come on, I'd watch my wife's eyes. Even news of Zambia or South Africa or Mali or (later) areas in the Middle East sent spears of anxiety through me. Something told me that she longed to be there, away from me, and the rest was patience. Once Egypt itself was mentioned, something about an irrigation project. My wife caught me staring at her and stared back, smiling, as the newscaster's words broke over us like a swarm of flies. No sleep *that* night. Jennifer cooked, I helped, we sipped at chilled cheap wine. I watched my wife chopping cloves of garlic, I would scoop up a diamond of garlic and bite it between my teeth. Her black hair falling into her face, my wife looked beautiful. She hummed a song, something from the radio. She was virtually my prisoner now. Do prisoners sing like that? Or was she singing some Nile Delta blues number? I loved her and hated myself, a balanced conjunction, these days. Paul came in. We played in front of the empty Georgian fireplace, a hangover from when these multi-tenanted flats were once elegant townhouse rooms. Italian stucco on the ceilings and posters of Che Guevara on the walls; well, we'd come on from then. Jennifer and I had a battery of stereo speakers under the Neapolitan cherubim. That morning I had come upon a letter from Egypt in the mail and had fought with great effort against the desire – temptation is a weak word – to open it. Sooner or later, I knew, I'd start opening my wife's letters. Paul grinned up at me and made a face. I smoked a cigarette. The doorbell sounded. Patel beamed in, smiling, immaculately turbaned. Jennifer had cooked something determinedly spicy and hot. We conversed throughout the meal about the state of the country, whether it was any good to vote any more, and how it was that, in India and chiefly at weddings, people managed to die in large numbers by accident. Patel blamed poverty, and I agreed up to a point. Drowning tragedies are usually a result of greed on the part of boat owners, said Patel. Perhaps, I said. It all seems such a *foreign* way to die, in an overcrowded boat. My wife coughed. In Galway, said my wife slowly, in the early part of the last century, a goat put his foot through the bottom of a boat and people drowned. She looked from me to Patel, to her son Paul. To our son Paul. I believe there is a poem about it. Patel scrubbed his plate clean with a hunk of seeded bread and smiled. Cultures, cultures; it's all a question of the dark side of human nature, he said, emphasising it with a doll-like wag of his head. We all suffer from it, he added.

We drank a good deal, at least I did. Patel was moderate to the point of being infuriating. When he left around midnight I straightaway accused Jennifer of giving him the eye over dinner. She was, of course, appalled. She began to understand that her husband was turning into a fascist and a paranoiac. Between them, Patel and Jennifer, it seemed to me that I'd been given a fair degree of patronising chit-chat. They pitied me, the way humane people pity small dogs with fractured legs. Yes, yes, it was *obvious* that she'd have much more in common with Patel; he was, after all, a *stranger* like herself. I thought he was your friend, said my wife. Paul hugged her knees, her wonderful, wonderful long legs. My son looked up at me and shivered. Without realising it, I'd assumed a menacing attitude over them both. My whole being threatened them. Don't hit Mammy, my son said; and when I heard the words I knew a part of my life had ended. A part of *me* had ended. I straightened up, there was no more to say. Jennifer stared at me, through God knows what dark mists, and pronounced, slowly, the words I had never believed would ever be addressed to me: *You racist bastard.*

A week after the Patel escapade, Paul came home from school with a bruise on his cheek and scuffed knees. He was accompanied by an embarrassed and apologetic schoolteacher who swore that this sort of thing *never* happened in her school – *her* school, as opposed to *Paul's* school – and there was always the possibility that my son had fallen off the push-bike by accident and, well, we all know what children are like at making up stories. I told her Paul was not *children*, he was my son, and the big difference was he did not tell lies and he especially would not make up a lie about his classmates, little Christian angels that they undoubtedly were, calling him names like the ones he said they'd called him. Inwardly, I knew that the vehemence of my defence of Paul was in direct proportion to the disgust I felt at my own behaviour during Patel's visit, and my growing terror. I threatened to remove Paul from the school. The teacher stood up. She issued an odour of chalk and dryness. Do reconsider, she said, acknowledging Jennifer with a smile. Throughout the episode, my wife remained stolidly calm and silent. In bed that night she announced that she wanted to go home for a holiday. Of course she'd take Paul. My terror was such that it paralysed me. I threw things at the wall when morning came; I got drunk, threatened unspeakable domestic horrors. My wife did not lose her composure. She did not fear losing me. She feared, she said, losing herself. Losing also her son, to some nameless, altered behaviour to which her husband was now prey. You have driven me away, she said. But I love you, I protested. How? she asked. Tears in my eyes, I said: What do you mean, *how?*

I knew this holiday would last forever. Still drunk enough, I drove to the airport a few days later. She'd been saying goodbye to friends in secret for weeks, I discovered, and no one encouraged her to stay. Then I kissed my wife for the last time. There is no kiss on earth like it. It comes feverishly, with the knowledge that after it, one minute later, one hour later, that night, the next day, there will be no other to follow it. Other things determine the length of this horror; public address systems, digital clocks, the motion forward of a queue. Nothing belongs to you any more. The voice of God sends out a Final Boarding call. You are babbling. Every word must mean something. The kiss comes, you try to suck the person into yourself forever. One half-minute from the end of this kiss the person will, to all intents and purposes, cease to exist. They are, for you, no more. Nothing in your experience can comprehend this utter emptiness. Paul kissed me and Jennifer kissed me and I experienced two separate deaths; and then I experienced my own, and dying has never held much horror for me since. They were gone; the flat was empty, the rooms silent. Nothing is like this. The memory is a permanent scar on the heart. Nothing heals it.

Now I drive Paul to the airport. Things have improved. There is a chance Jennifer might visit, maybe next year. Official separation was a question of formality. Paul is curious about a girl I introduced him to. He wants to know if I like her as much as I like his mother. At the airport I hand him over to the trained gentleness of a pretty stewardess. He is laden with books, model aircraft kits, dressed in a yuppie pair of denims. I kiss him. Be good to your Mammy, I say. He says nothing. He has learned, at partings, to make no promises, no last remarks, things that might be remembered. If the plane falls out of the sky, I will remember forever his last silence.

I hand him a final present, a pair of marble earrings for his mother. God knows if she'll wear them. He smiles, my son. He takes the pretty girl's hand and disappears. I turn back towards the city where I am a native, where my prejudices drift and fall like leaves, according to winds blown up before I was born. I remember the street, the outside of the clinic where I first met my wife. I was happy there. My mother still refers to Paul as *that girl's child*, as if I had nothing to do with it and, worse, Jennifer was a casual stranger. I turn my car down the ramp towards the heart of my country. I drive among the things which made me what I am.

Toledo

The carriage was so hot by now that even the windows seemed to sweat. Two young servicemen, the top buttons of their tunics undone, sat across from them, caught in a steady triangle of white sunlight. Through the window the plain turned yellow and white by turns; and the man in the grey loose-fitting business suit kept on talking.

'You like Madrid?'

He had made the mistake of mentioning Madrid. Where they had been, what they had visited. The conversation had become one-sided and dreary, a mixture of heat and mental effort. There was a vague feeling of unease, as if someone were about to apologise for something. He looked at her profile and saw that she was looking at the young servicemen and he felt an old unformed jealousy, something inadequate about himself. He wished the man would stop talking, would let him sleep.

'It's a big city.'

The man smiled. The carriage rocked and bumped suddenly, then calmed down. There was the thick heavy odour of black tobacco and the man exhaled smoke into the stifled atmosphere once again.

'Big and very bad to live there.'

Perhaps this was a question. She turned her face to him and he was struck as he never failed to be by her uncompromising beauty; the wide dark eyes, the skin which required no make-up, the frame of dark straight hair. Why, he wondered, why did I ever take you off your island?

'You have not seen Spain if you have only seen Madrid. Madrid is for business only. All tourists. You have been to the Prado? You have seen "Guernica"? Yes? But that is nothing. I was born in a small town. Now I go to Madrid only for the business.'

'The Retiro is a lovely place. We took a boat out on the lake last week.'

'The Retiro is full of young people drinking at night and sleeping and drugs.'

Her face was beautiful, surely. And in her tiny room, high above the Atlantic, a wet winter closing on them both with arms of shivering frost, she had recited some lines from that Joyce story, 'The Dead'.

Something oblique about knowing that love was when someone was willing to say they'd die for you. He had smiled to himself that evening; leaving her with a quick kiss, he had been overcome with a sense of dread, as if she were about to leave him or had hinted that she might. But she had not died for him and he had not died for her. But he had taken her away from the cold, he thought, and brought her with a crump of wheels down on the slithery tarmac of Barajas airport under a scorched blue sky and light that tore at their northern eyes. For two days she had spoken hardly a word. He saw that she was frightened, on unfamiliar territory, out of her depth, and one night she had dreamed fitfully in her sleep beside him and called out something in her native Irish.

'Aranjuez', the man in the loose suit said.

I will show you the world, Catherine, he had said. But per-haps she did not need to see the world. Perhaps all she wanted was him. It was hardly enough. So he was showing her the world.

The train slowed down and the brakes whistled and Aranjuez station was sand-coloured brickwork and peeling paint and rusting girders and a clock so big it might have rolled out of a Dali painting. Aranjuez. Rodrigo's Concerto. He didn't see anything inspiring in the drab hot station. His eyes strained against the light and he caught her faint odour of sweat and wanted, in that exhausted moment, to put his arms round her shoulders and pull her to him, to have her dissolve into him. But the man in the suit said something about strawberries.

'When I was much younger, naturally. Every Sunday. The train came from Madrid and that is what it was called, the Strawberry Train. White wine and strawberries. Aranjuez is a very beautiful place. But we have no time.'

He looked the man full in the face and ignored his hapless smiling stare. Clean-shaven, sweating under the white open-collared shirt. A successful man in a modest way. Fortyish, maybe. A Spaniard who had worked at his English with the avidness of someone looking for the key to unlock a personal prison, perhaps. A country boy, dying of provincialism and growing aware of the world. Under Franco, then, of course. Spain the outpost of Europe. It must have been necessary to dream very quietly. Or maybe he was a Franco man and regretted the general's demise; who cared? The carriage echoed with the sound of women's excited voices and a haggle over seating arrangements. Every seat was numbered and where one sat was a matter of precise importance. Then the train moved out of Aranjuez station and plunged south again over the chequered yellow plain under the intolerable relentlessness of blue.

That man is very vulgar, she had said, having stared blindly at Fernando Botero's fat-assed nudes in the gallery of the Reina Sofia. There is something funny about his paintings, but I still think he's unnecessarily vulgar. But you don't think James Joyce was vulgar, he had countered. James Joyce is dead, she said. This man has exhibited all over Europe, he told her; they

had been walking along the Gran Via and a thunderstorm had
been gathering over the mountains. He had taken her to a café
and bought her milky *horchatas*, two of them one after the
other. He made a crack about a brand of gin named Focking
and she had cleared her throat and patted his hand; that's vulgar too. When the storm finally broke she had clung to him,
both of them deserted-looking and suddenly cold as they
searched for a taxi. The lightning and the thunder frightened
her. He loved her for the child she was and mistrusted the awkward, stumbling woman. But when he had first walked with
her under the ruined walls of Dún Aonghus he had been
attracted by this stumbling, had fallen in love with her broad
innocent smile and the hidden knowledge of the world she pro-
fessed to conceal under that girlish wet-lipped pout. One grew
to hate the things one had once loved. Irony is often bitter; in
the Metro he had kissed her and wiped away her unexpected
tears and the train had broken into their intimacy with a roar
and a rush of air and the hydraulic impersonality of doors
opening. Just then he would have given all of Spain for her little room, her soft opening mouth, the scent of the roses he had
sent her, the odour of her sweat and his own and the darkness
of the Atlantic night. But they were underground, surrounded
by Madrid and Spain, and smothered under twinned anxieties.
Now the man in the suit stubbed out his cigarette and sought
about for his ticket. The ticket-inspector leaned over them in a
dark suit and cleaved the brightness of the carriage in two.

'*Donde vas?*'

'Toledo.'

'*Gracias. Por favor…*'

'They don't speak Spanish.'

The inspector ignored the man in the suit. He stood over
both of them like a sweating archangel and held out his hand;
the tickets were inspected, plugged, returned. He disappeared.

'I forget my own language,' the man said, smiling as if the
smile obsessed him.

'Almost to you I said: *No voy jamás a Madrid en agosto,* which is true, but you wouldn't understand. I think my English is very good, no?'

'I think it is excellent.'

'Spanish is easy. Can you speak any of Spanish?'

'No, I'm afraid not.'

'And your *novia*?'

'I'm sorry?'

'This word means your friend. *Qué buena estas, señorita.*'

'No. I'm afraid neither of us speaks Spanish.'

'You have read Lorca?'

Then, back in the hotel, the cramps in her stomach had distressed him into a virtually interminable panic. Using frustrating sign-language, he had obtained from a chemist a greenish bottle of something which had purged his *novia* of her pain. *Novia*. The word hinted at 'novena', or something holy, sacrosanct. It sounded vaguely like the Latin for the number nine. On the island, on her beloved island, when he had begun to tire of silence and contemplation and all the things he had sought after for years, he had made love to her almost against her wishes. He thought about this now and felt the gathering of a vague guilt. She had been a virgin. She had wept and refused to speak to him until an hour before he was due to get the plane back to Galway. Then she had walked him down to the pub in Kilronan, and he, consulting his wristwatch nervously, had heard her tell him she loved him. I love you too, Catherine; the plane slid upwards into a musty grey afternoon and belted back up Galway Bay as if the mutual declarations frightened it. There was no true sanity anymore after that. Letters, phone-calls. Come away with me. A holiday. I see right through you to the limitless peace of God. You symbolise for me all that is worth saving in our wretched country. Your innocence is all I require. When we make love our bodies write verses of poetry on the sheets. Catherine Catherine Catherine. He had gone quite mad. The letters verged on the pornographic. He heard her disapproval and sensed her paradoxical intense desire on the 'phone. Like a thief he had stolen her from the island. But she had existed only on the island. Away from it, she had stopped breathing. She had left her soul in safe-keeping under a smooth stone somewhere near Kilronan. Now, around her white unsunned neck, a bright silver cross glinted and swung as if to remind him of his sin.

The man in the suit indicated the young servicemen with a discreet nod of his head.

'Under Franco, my father fought. He was a soldier and very young. He had no question to ask. He did not like Franco very much. But he was in the army.'

'Of course.'

'*Sí.* That is.'

'Were you in the army too, under Franco?'

'*Sí. Me cagüen los soldados.* They are all *condenados. La pobrecita,* your *novia.* She is tired?'

Yes, he thought quickly; she is tired of me, finally, and will not say it. She will not say that she is only my dream, and that as a real person she walks even now on the stones of Inishmore. God, I love her; but that's never an excuse for anything.

'I'm fine, really.'

Her tired, aching, beautiful soft voice. He loved her words as they floated out into the clammy air, he loved their dips and hollows. She spoke so little these days; since touching down at Barajas, she had spoken only to criticise or plead. He had broken something in her that he could never put together again. Maybe she had died for him after all, and he hadn't noticed. One gets so confused, he told himself. The train squealed as if in pain. He looked over the shoulders of the young soldiers and saw Toledo rise like a pale yellow wart on the dry skin of the plain. It was veiled in heat and beautiful to look at. She looked where he looked. But he could no longer be sure of what she saw. He had promised them both this trip because a week in Madrid and they'd both felt the onset of tears. Toledo; he had persuaded her of its usefulness, as he had persuaded her of Spain and of himself.

The dream of Spain had been his dream and had nothing to do with her, with Catherine, with islands surrounded by the sea and their pitiless silences. In the Puerta del Sol a blind man churned a hurdy-gurdy to the apologetic clink of glinting pesetas; he had photographed her, his sturdy island girl, her smile like a rising sun, against this carnival conception of Spain. She had enveloped him in the hot narrow bed of the siesta, while outside the Guadarrama veiled its soft gradients under a white heat. No, he had not read Lorca and knew or cared little of Franco. But the buses snapped and murmured beneath their tired single window and drew out the afternoon like great individual ticks of an almighty clock. And he ran his fingers down the fragile spine of her back and she twitched suddenly in her sleep and he had seen then how vulnerable she was, how miraculously beautiful and taut as a finely-tuned string. O Catherine, I have sinned grievously against thee! In my callous ignorance, in my desire for mastery. And I am heartily sorry.

'Toledo,' said the man in the suit, who cursed soldiers, leaning far out in the aisle and straining to see the town rise up smoky and glorious, like a relished memory. He pursed his lips and began whistling a tune. The young servicemen buttoned their tunics and smoothed themselves down. Women's voices cackled and rose. The heat in the carriage was like a slap in the face.

In the cool splendour of the Circulo de Bellas Artes she had drawn her fingers over the delicate marble curves of the sculptured nude in the lounge, while he had scribbled hasty postcards home and watched her, scrutinised her, and the immaculate waiters fluttered like doves bearing trays of fragrant teas and beer and sticky coffee and the ubiquitous horchatas. She had curled up beside him on the soft leather couch; around them, city men read *El Pais* and young elegantly-dressed women showed their bronze legs and sighed and smoked cigarettes. As they emerged from the old club, across the street a wedding party tumbled down a flight of steps from a discreet church and the bride exploded in a blaze of white. All around them the city of Madrid honked and sputtered and rumbled like a protesting goliath cursed with colic. And they could never, it seemed, escape Madrid's interminable babble and throng, and she had developed stomach cramps, and he had nursed her fretfully and with an increasing feeling of guilt. But now the shape of Toledo cleaned itself up and he saw that she looked at the turning fortress as the train manoeuvred to the west. I hope you love me, she had whispered as they linked arms coming out of the Circulo; I hope you love me as I love you.

'A hot day. Buy a hat in Toledo.'

'I will.'

'I am very serious. It is too hot.'

'I will. I promise.'

The man in the suit, a symbol he would forever identify with a vague pain left of and below his heart, grew more intense about the purchase of a hat as Toledo became a brick reality and emerged out of the husky dustiness of the plain.

'We Spaniards have a tolerance of the sun. Not you. A hat is significant.'

'I can appreciate that and I will follow your advice.'

'*Sí.*'

The train bucked and shuddered and slowed, and the women and the servicemen and the man in the suit shifted themselves in sudden searches for items of luggage. Then the train entered the station and squealed to a stop. The doors hissed apart. They were out on the platform and then they were being pushed into the station, into a building whose ornamentation was so elaborate that it might have been a converted mosque. The servicemen disappeared; but the man in the suit showed up again at the bus-stop. Toledo itself towered over them now and seemed to smile. The heat was very great and pressed down on his head like a hot towel. She held his hand and shouldered her small rucksack. Put on your sunglasses, he told her; the glare is terrible. She did as he told her. He kissed the top of her head and felt how hot her black hair had become and smelled that wonderful child's smell of oiled hair and natural sweat. The bus came and they bundled aboard, shoving and uncertain. The man in the suit waved them into two seats.

'*Por favor*. Sit.'

It was her silence which tormented him most, which aggravated his guilt and robbed him of hope. He could have endured an outburst, a stinking row; but her silence wore away at his soul with the persistence of water dripping on stone. Maybe I will explode, he thought as the bus pulled up the steep gradient into the town; maybe I will break down and weep and be taken away by polite strangers. Maybe I will leave her to fend for herself. Maybe I will wait until she is asleep and strangle her and when they ask me why I did it I will say I did it for love.

He looked out of the window and upwards to the stubborn completeness of the Alcázar. He recalled the story of General Moscardó's defence of the place at the start of the Civil War, holding out there, surrounded by his civil guards and cadets against the Republicans until the Nationalists relieved him from Seville; the bus arched its back in preparation for the advance on the Alcázar and he wondered what had become of Gerald Brenan's little book, where he'd stowed it away, and for a brief moment he became obsessed with the notion of uncovering its whereabouts. He drew upon mental geographies, he sorted and sifted through possibilities. He concluded that the book lay snug and safe at the very bottom of Catherine's neat rucksack, as if buried out of spite where he could not reach it.

But for the Spain into which he had pressed them both there were no guidebooks, no reminiscences. No one had been here before, so no one knew the territory. He glanced down at her knees, shapely, slim, pressed together in her only pair of faded denim jeans. When she wore the jeans it was almost an attempt to become someone else for him, a change of skin. He had no such devices and felt he was growing intolerably old. The bus gave out that Toledo was not built for engines and diesel-driven machinery; it growled that the mistress of Lope de Vega, languishing away in the impossible heat, had been tricked; it muttered something vague about St Teresa writing letters to the world upon these same cobbles. But what of St John of the Cross, the poems that rose to heaven, that carried the soul upon wings of love towards the Ultimate Love? The bus was lulling him to sleep amid bookish recollections and half-construed memories of things heard, gleaned from postcards and pamphlets. His Spain had sunk into pulp and photographs. His head rested heavily against her shoulder; he could not even be sure that she still breathed, her silence was so clean and total. What of the legend that the Toledo Jews were consulted at the time of Christ's trial, and they recommended his release; their communiqué to Jerusalem had arrived too late, and their magnanimity had not changed the world. The diesel fumes entered the body of the bus and the women's voices rose. Speak to me, one word of absolution. Toledo was suspended over the river gorges as if it had attempted to rise to heaven on one of St John's poems. He pulled himself upright in the seat and saw the plain behind him glimmer and shake. In the crowded streets, a modern bank jostled for architectural space beside a tiny artisan's shop above the door of which an ancient coat-of-arms simmered in the sunlight. Tourists everywhere. The cyclopean swing of cameras. She cleared her throat and he mistook the sound for a word; he smiled and turned to her, but she remained silent. He saw how long her eyelashes were and how sad her eyes had become. Something is burning inside me, Catherine; something I cannot extinguish, a fierce fire of hopelessness and solitude. I have been cast out of the holy city of your heart. I am on the outskirts, under the walls, begging. El Cid. Who was it? Charlton Heston. Aranjuez and the Strawberry Train. Rodrigo's Concerto again. Da-da-da! Dam-dam-dam-dam-dam-dam-dam – da-da-da! Here we both are. A bus arguing its way up the hillside, crossing the Puente de Alcantara with the Tajo below, olive trees in neat rows; the island of her childhood and of her heart long ago dissolved into colder latitudes, a weatherbeaten dream. The very first photograph I ever took of you in Spain was outside the little Baroque church beside the Prado. Sunlight blinded you, so you lifted your hand and shielded your eyes and the angels above the door flapped their wings to cool you. Inside, the carved saints wore real clothes. You stared at them, Catherine, and took up dry conversations with their plaster-and-stone austerities. They followed you with their eyes; and a mysterious and invisible loft organ played something from Handel; hadn't Haydn written for Holy Week in Seville? Outside we were still excited by sound, colour, the new textures of Madrid. We had not yet looked to ourselves, or become aware of the dissolution of ourselves in the heat, in the grotesque subtlety of gathered anxieties and misgivings. Velásquez and his funny little court dwarves; a sensitive man, seeing life as it was, not as convention dictated; nothing was hidden, even the absurd, the neglected, given a throne upon which to display themselves. Not so with us. Our anguish concealed itself in the shadows of our bedroom silences. We had no Velásquez to render visible the private tortures, the unseemly postures of the helpless.

'*Tienes fuego, por favor? Gracias, Senor. Ai! Agosto! Qué calor! Gracias.*'

The man in the suit thanked someone profusely for a light for yet another dark-smelling cigarette. Yes, August was a hot month to be anywhere in Spain. Toledo scratched its venerable gables in the appalling windless heat. They'd come up from the river and the bridge, they'd negotiated the first awkward streets, they'd marvelled at the variety of tourists and the snap of the engine's heavy gears as the bus-driver sought one last inspirational effort of horse-power to pull the vehicle upwards towards the safety of the Alcázar. He was still on the train; he was still peering out of the bus into the Tajo; he was cradling her head on his lap as the jet bounded downwards towards La Mancha and someone, terrified at the steps-and-stairs descent and its rapidity, had screeched from the back of the aircraft: '*Me cagüen tu puta madre!*' intended for the pilot. Then he was inching through Toledo, and he remembered her Thank You and sudden impromptu kiss on his mouth when he purchased a rose for her in the middle of the night from a pretty rose-seller in Madrid. An act of almost sacred determination; he would show her just how absolutely he loved her, he would speak in symbols. *Mi corazón,*

Catherine. Now he felt the child's pressure of her fingers tighten on his arms; they had grown old together, they had fallen overboard and neither could swim, let alone save the other. When we get home I will show you how much I love you, he thought.

The bus strained and rattled and climbed into Toledo and the great plain opened up behind them and he could see the train lines like a thin pencil-scratch going North to Madrid. Atocha Station, where, in among the steaming rusting tracks, he had seen a man, half naked, standing on his head on a cement plinth in a yoga position while around him trains hurtled and screamed and clattered under their power-lines and shunted in the sidings. And above Madrid, like a symbol of God, the tower of the broadcasting station had shone with the holy fire of the La Mancha sun.

But they were in Toledo now. The streets were too narrow, the traffic moved with the impatient caution of drunks. No one wanted to fall off Toledo into the plain. Street signs were in Arabic, English, Yiddish, Spanish; a town of Moors, bustling Jews, Christians with Inquisitions in their eyes. And El Greco making a name for himself. The Tajo river flowed bright yellow beneath the walls of the town. The town had been declared a national monument. The Alcázar sang quietly of civil wars and dungeons. The bus lurched exhaustedly into the Calle de Capuchinos and then everyone disembarked. The man in the suit kissed her chivalrously on the cheek and shook his hand.

'*Buenas tardes. 'Luego.*'

They bought a guidebook and he took her to the church of Santo Tomé to see El Greco's famous *Burial of the Count of Orgaz*. A guide mustered them into a group of Japanese and Americans and described El Greco's life in a quarter of an hour and the famous painting, which threatened them all from a wall just inside the church, in an even shorter space of time. And there was the painter himself, bearded, a self-made man with a townhouse in Toledo, staring out at his public, his son beneath him and in his son's pocket a handkerchief with the painter's name inscribed on it. Conceit. And the nobles looked up to heaven and the grey-faced sainted Count appeared about to open his eyes and laugh. The heat in the church was sickening and she tugged at his sleeve and made a vomiting face. Outside in the cobbled street he held her to him and looked into her eyes. Are you alright, Catherine? Fine, she assured him, I'll be fine. It's the heat. They strolled from gift shop to gift shop with the sun on their heads like anointing fire. The armour and the souvenir swords carried blinding weights of sunlight. He longed for rest, as if he had made an unrewarding and spiritless pilgrimage and found the holy shrine turned into a hamburger stall. They patrolled the dead, narrow, tepid streets in utter silence, as if silence had enveloped them and refused to go. They passed a party of Andalucían gypsies, elegant and formally dressed in stiff black. The thin man doffed his hat respectfully and addressed the stooped black-scarfed old woman with incredible defiant courtesy, and as they passed *the* scene he heard the words: '*Doña Maria Angelína Concepción – buenas tardes.*'

He did not look behind, but hurried on, desperate now for shade, for drinks, for sleep. He purchased cheap enamels and silver inscribed 'Toledo' key-rings; she bought him a tiny silver sword and he kissed her and bought her a headscarf with a map of Toledo printed on it. He produced his camera and photographed her against a backdrop of cliffs and the sluggish waters of the Tajo. They found a café and sat down in it and watched the motorcyclists race each other down the narrow streets as if El Greco had never existed. A party of Orthodox Jews waded solemnly through the little white tables and disappeared into a rickety street. He bought a packet of cigarettes and she helped him smoke one. They ate a fat sandwich and drank light golden bottled beer which calmed them down, or seemed to. The cold liquid burned a hole in the back of his throat and he relaxed a little. By now Toledo surrounded them as Madrid had done. The heat was heavy and molten and they seemed to breathe in whole lungfuls of sunlight. Suddenly he wanted to weep and started into another cigarette, dumbfounded at his lapse into what he interpreted as a kind of moral weakness; this was not how Spain had been meant to be, and it was falling down around his ears and O Catherine! Is it all going to die of exhaustion here in Toledo?

They walked down towards the Tajo, towards the great cliffs and the sandy gates and the patient bridges of stone. His legs were heavy and tired and he looked at her from time to time as much to reaffirm that she was still with him as anything else. The thought that he might look and discover that she had evaporated into thin air filled him with terror. I will make it right back home, he told himself. We will survive our silence, the silence that Spain and my stupidity has cursed us with, and we will make it all right again back home in the friendly familiar rain.

They stood on the bridge under the shadow of the Puente de San Martín. He turned to take a photograph of her, of his wonderful Catherine, framed by the ancient stone gate and ennobled under the historic emblazonry and coats-of-arms. But she had thrown down her rucksack and was leaning back against the stonework with her hands over her face. He ran to her, his camera dangling like a severed head. He pulled and pulled but she would not take her hands from her face. Then she seemed to disintegrate in front of him, the words in her native Irish slamming into his heart, his scorched guilty soul, until he could barely manage to avoid the swipes she made at his face with her clenched little fists. Her face had been made ugly by tears and screaming. He could say nothing, heard her accusations and had no defence. He stepped back on to the bridge and heard her sobbing slow and ease out behind him. I hope you love me as I love you. Beneath him the waters of the Tajo giggled and muttered something about dying for love and all around him the deep song of an ineffable loneliness rose up and deafened him.

(For Joaquin Roncero del Pino)

Northern Star

Shall I be gentle? Generous? Shall I merely sit and listen? A lovely evening for a stroll on the promenade; dogs yapping and couples holding hands, a warm breeze, a moon coming up, the bay calm as glass. Smell of salt and ammonia. Lights like jewellery. She talks on and I watch her over the rim of my glass.

'You despise us both.'

'No,' I say. 'That's unfair and quite wrong.'

'But what can you think of two people who endure this sort of thing?'

'I think he's unwell. I think he's lost control.'

'Ah! Well, if you want to talk about *control*...'

I look at her, the big blue eyes, dark wavy hair, plump but attractive figure, and wonder how long I have known her. I too have acquired crow's feet. And I'm probably plump now, too. How long? And how long have I known him? A dozen years, maybe. And we have changed, altered, in those barely perceptible ways which count for so much. Which add up, almost always, to something quite big and inexplicable. Where he had once merely disagreed with her at parties and in pubs, now he beat her. The dark grey ring beneath her left eye made her look slightly sinister and weighted one side of her face. A very pretty face. She telephones me and I go to her. She asks me to tell her stories about what she calls *the old days*, when we were all in our twenties, when nothing was either scared or serious, when hope was possible. The stories relieve the agony she feels, I guess, at having become a statistic. He is not a bad man; this is not, ever, a moral issue. I believe that. In any case, when drunk, he beats her. And I hate him for it but do not despise them in the way she believes I do. Do I love her? No; once, perhaps, but no longer. Too much emotion spent elsewhere in between. But there is a great affection.

Now, wearing denim jeans and a loose white V-neck sweater over pert breasts, she moves towards the window in bare feet, bearing a glass of Black and White. When she looks out over the crisp lawns and the dark trees towards the bay, God knows what she thinks or sees there.

She sips, her lips wet with whiskey. An attractive woman with a black eye.

'Are we still your pet Northerners?'

I'd called them this when they first made the move from Belfast to this seaside town on the west coast. It was a term of affection which, somehow, she had always regarded with suspicion; as if some deeper and less agreeable connotation lay simmering quietly beneath its surface. But now it was a flag held out, a signal, and some recognition was required.

'Yes, very much so. Is that OK?'

'The first time you said that about us, called us that, I thought you were being sarcastic, or cynical, or something.'

'No. Nothing like that.' Was that the truth? She turns from the window and behind her, as if at her sign, the moon rose a full inch further. How much had I ever known about them, their backgrounds, their beliefs? She read poetry and he worked in a solicitor's office off Royal Avenue. I worked on a small innocent fashion magazine which lasted six months and folded. We drank in The Crown, opposite the Europa Hotel, and when the night was good enough we ate first at an Italian restaurant; these were the good days, in truth. They didn't last. Bad things happened. My job no longer existed, I took to looking elsewhere: nothing. The city was a cold place without money and they allowed me to borrow from them. I hated it. It did something very odd and regrettable to the friendship. They lived, newly wed, in a four-room flat off the Ormeau Road. On Sundays we walked in Ormeau Park, in among the trees, down the slopes. Belfast Sunday quietness has nothing to match it into the world. God at rest. Then I went for an interview one weekend into this western town, took a bus across the Border and over the deadly solitude of the Irish Midlands, as impassive as a graveyard, into Cromwell's Siberia. And I suppose that, more or less, at the same hour – I was unpacking my single travelling-bag in a boarding-house, a picture of the crucified Christ in the hallway over the telephone and the welcoming odour of frying and the hearty sound of a radio disc-jockey introducing Country 'n' Western music – at more or less this same hour, they were both blown into the air coming out of a cinema on their way for a late drink. I got the job in the West, advertising consultant to a large boutique chain. When I got back to Belfast they were in the hospital, shaken, otherwise unhurt. Three other people had died, blown all over the place. They moved south. I met my wife in this town, a lovely, spirited girl. They attended our wedding. My wife and I are happy people but we cannot live together. So a couple of years ago we went our separate ways. We meet regularly, give one another dinner, have a few drinks. Thank God we managed to retain affection for one another, for I loved her dearly and probably still do.

'Tell me about Spain.'

I begin, with protestations, the reminiscences about the holiday the four of us took in Madrid; the Prado, the old man selling bracelets and medallions with photographs of Franco in them, the organ-grinder in the Puerta de Sol, the intolerable midday heat and the transvestites in the sidewalk cafés in the humid wee morning hours. My wife brought statuettes of Sancho Panza and Don Quixote which, she said, reflected the two sides of the Spanish nature. We watched a bullfight on television in a stifling bar, sawdust on the floor: the whole time we were there I read Aidan Higgins' *Balcony of Europe*. At night my wife and I made love on the cool tiles of our rented apartment floor. In the room next to ours, the fighting would begin. 'You stupid whore!' he'd say. In those days, before immunity set in, she would cry loudly.

I tell the stories of Spain which are tolerable; I say nothing of what my wife and I, sated with our love-making and drenched in sweat, sat bolt upright and listened to above the low din of Madrid's all-night traffic.

'Those were the days,' she says. She has a certain look, a way of directing her eyes that indicates how miserable she can feel. The look materialises now. She is, perhaps, getting a little comfortably drunk. We have been sitting here for almost an hour. Outside, evening has come down like a soft fall of soot through which the moon and the points of promenade light manage to peek. 'Yes,' she says. 'Your pet Northerners. He's impotent, you know.'

'That's none of my business.'

'Well, he *is*. Can't manage the job at all. Makes a fool of himself.'

'Do you think it's funny? You say it as if you do.'

'No,' she says then, her lilting accent dropping a tone or two, as if feeling my slight polite reprimand. 'It's anything but funny.'

I smoke a cigarette. The smoke curls greyly towards their decorated plasterwork. Decanters on the sideboard; framed prints. A rack full of classical records and a record-player, old-fashioned type, in a corner. As a solicitor, word has it that he's good enough, competent. He is given credit for his pragmatism. As long as I've known him he has not once displayed one ounce of so-called Ulster Calvinist common sense; she dresses like a little girl being readied for Sunday school whenever they go out, white gloves, wide-brimmed hat. He is a sloppy dresser, always bad with money, rash, a boozer, a wife-beater. Neither Calvinism nor being of good Antrim planter stock has saved him from being a gross failure. He has, on the other hand, managed to marry a woman who will probably drink herself to death rather than leave him.

Have I any right to say these things? Have I any right to *think* them? They have filled my days; they have been friends to me, companions when misery overtook me. Indeed, when poverty itself threatened to drag me under. Yet they are cowards, both of them. Beyond redemption, I would think. The blast in Belfast; it did something to them, too early on in their marriage. It scared them. Childless still and – if what she says is true – threatened further by his impotence and his drunken violence, they are a standing tribute to the blindness of societal manners and keeping up a good front. But she trusts me.

'Do you and Yvonne sleep together?'

'Occasionally.'

'Jesus! That's how it *should* be. Civilised. Want another drink?'

'No thanks.'

'Well you'll not mind if I have one.'

She pours, adding ice. She shakes the glass vigorously and stands over me, wearing a scolded little girl pout. She is more than simply attractive in this half light, in the light of his ill-treatment of her, in the bright light of my own loneliness and my discarded love for Yvonne, my lovely wife. ' I lie beside him and think of you,' she says. 'That is, I think of you and a hundred other men I pass in the street every day, not necessarily you particularly. Don't get all strange because I said that. It's natural enough.'

I don't know what to say. I stare into my glass and wonder what it would be like to drown in whiskey, or even in the sea. Once, drunk in a café-bar in Madrid, I spent a half-hour watching a tiny fly drown in a glass of wine.

She runs her hand through her hair; dandruff floats into the air and vanishes. She shakes her head vigorously. She gulps down a big mouthful of whiskey and turns away, smiling vaguely, half to herself, half to me.

'You'd go to bed with me in a second if you thought you wouldn't be found out,' she says.

'I have no one to find me out.'

'Your prickly little Roman Catholic conscience would find you out,' she says, staring once more out through the window into the night and the waters of the bay. For an instant I remember the agonised face of Christ over the 'phone in the boarding-house; symbols, emblems, tokens, provoking a guilt at the back of the intellect that runs as deep as childhood. When had I lost my faith? At the same time as I lost my marriage, frankly.

'Please don't flirt with me.'

'Because it makes you uncomfortable?'

'Because, yes, it does. You know it does.'

'It would be like going to bed with an old friend,' she says.

'That's precisely what it *would* be,' I say. 'And it would be no use to either of us. We don't need that.'

'Speak for your bloody self,' she says.

What had the car-bomb done to *her*? What were these immeasurable after-effects? What part of her had been blown away forever that night in Belfast? What part of *him*? For a moment or two she seems to have locked her gaze into the infinite horizon; a distance beyond the bay, beyond the mountains, beyond the world itself. She remains as if hypnotised by the cold vagueness of the dark beyond the window; or something out there which is visible only for her. A memory? She turns to me and her eyes glisten in the semi-darkness. 'Please forgive me,' she says, and then turns back to staring out of the window.

On a cushion near the fireplace, a copy of an early collection of poems by John Hewitt. On a shelf above the record-player, an autographed photo of a prominent Northern Irish film-actor. He was younger then. Queen's University. Hushed lawns, raucous Students' Union, Civil Rights, Burntollet. The sparrows fussed loudly round the green dome of City Hall and

baton-charged one another. Newspaper photographs of stream-
ing head-wounds. A taxi driven at high speed down the Antrim
Road, the three of us drunk as lords, the taxi-driver their land-
lord also. Drinking gin out of the bottle in a taxi-office in the
Short Strand. B-Specials, rubber bullets, housing action cam-
paigns; steadily he practised law, steadily she wrote her wee
hard poems, published them in university magazines long after
she'd abandoned university. Hard to let go. Umbilical. Lonely.

Neither of them ever involved in anything more serious
than organising quiet or not-so-quiet piss-ups, Northern Ireland spun around them, but they, like all true survivors,
remained untouched, disinterested, above and beyond it all. 'It's
a working-class battle,' he'd said to me in a snug in The Crown
one wet Friday evening; I always will remember that. 'So,' he
concluded, 'what the hell have the like of you or me to do with
it, eh?'

I tried to say something. I think I found that I had a need to
explain something very obvious to him. But he wouldn't listen,
waved his hand, shook his head, eyes-down, beyond reach. So
we remained sitting on the fence. And that was fair enough. Life
went on. Until the blast shook both of them out of a bubble
they had inflated around themselves. They had been, up to that
point, the untouchable ones. God was in His heaven and every
day was Sunday; not so, the voice of the bomb had told them;
not so. We are all victims, it is quite indiscriminate, death is not
prejudiced. Icy shoulder-touch. I think he began cracking open
then, like an egg.

A soft warm fireglow on the papered walls; subtle scent of
lavender, of something she'd sprayed on her neck and shoulders. Tang of cigarettes. A settee with comfortable armchairs;
reminiscent of Belfast parlours where the dead were laid out and
rectors treated to tea and scones. McVitie's biscuits, slices of
Hovis. A brass-potted plant with leathery leaves. She could not
get the finicky Northerner out of her system; it clung to everything she touched, or had ever touched, like a thin film. She
could not adapt to this seaside town, its bluntness, its music, or

its croquet-on-the-lawn lack of something. I knew she did not socialise. All her time here, and few friends, no close ones. He was the same, his situation redeemed somewhat by business associates, solicitors steeped in the tedium of generations of solicitors, a fathers-and-sons profession. No. He was everyone's pet Northerner. That he didn't share their religion either made him all the more open to being patronised. And – most hideous form of patronising – he had occasional affairs, women whose own marriages weren't sound, who had Sunday dinner at their parents' table, who dressed expensively and drank as he did. Now and then she attempted to write poems again; little came of it, there was too much unhappiness. She clears her throat, looks at her bare feet, curls her toes. Clipped nails.

'You remember in those old Victorian novels, the way girls married for convenience? Well, it's not just Victorian novels. I guess that's what happened to me.'

I listen. Outside, the sound of tyres on gravel. She does not look up. Yes, I think; I suppose it is. A good match, the prim young prudish daughter and the rising legal star, conservative also; untouchable, both. Why not? Curtained windows of university flat-land; music of Bob Dylan, Donovan, Hendrix. Carlos Castenada and Germaine Greer; pints of Tuborg lager and bottles of Monk Export. Skirt drawn to cover the knee; sit at the edge of the chair, knees together. White gloves. On Saturdays he'd be at a rugby match in Ravenhill with the boys. While she shopped in Anderson and McAuleys, Robbs, took her mother to Robinson and Cleavers and bought her a new hat for Sundays. 'Tailors to the King'. Yes, that's what happened. Love sanitised; but he'd been to bed with her somewhere or other after a Students' Union disco. Flaw. He'd told me years ago. While Derry burned. Another world.

'Yes, I guess that's what happened to me. Shocked? You should be. You and your Yvonne believed in love, didn't you? I think that's sadder.'

'You loved each other too,' I say, in the hope of redeeming something; but know, horribly, that it's probably not true.

'There must have been something to start with.'

'He was very good in bed. I knew nothing, he knew everything. Were you and Yvonne good in bed?'

I think back and the answer is my wheat-haired freckly wife was wonderful. What was wonderful was our mutual tenderness. Even when our petty difficulties overcame us, the tenderness remained. I realise how very fortunate I am, we both are. Sitting there sipping good whiskey, I knew Yvonne and I might get together again, some time in the future when we are too old for scepticism and in desperate need of tenderness again.

'We loved one another, that's true enough,' I say. 'Now, I have a distinct feeling that Roy's on his way up.'

'Pissed.'

'No doubt. I don't want to look like I was summoned here behind his back.'

'He knows I'll have called you.'

'He knows we talk like this?'

'He knows that *I* talk like this. He's not in the least bit jealous. He *trusts* you. He thinks that, in the end, you'll patch everything up nice and tidy between us if it comes to it. Roy's no longer in the real world.'

But I stand up nonetheless. Roy is a hefty man. I am his friend, but I won't meet him sitting down. We are silent, she and I, and listen for footsteps. None. Silence. Perhaps he's looking through the keyhole; who knows whether he trusts me with his drinking wife, drinking also. But their apartment door has no keyhole that anyone can look through. We are standing looking at each other in the middle of the room. We look at odd areas of each other's faces, avoiding the eyes at all costs; we are both so intolerably vulnerable here, in this room. At last she moves away, taking the comforting odour of lavender with her. I put my glass down on a glass-topped square coffee table and see that, under the top, there is a copy of the *Sunday Telegraph* and an opened box of Kleenex. Somewhere in their personal photo-albums, family treasures going back a hundred years, there are pictures of proud young men in uniform.

'Funny thing is,' she says with a throaty snigger, 'we were taught to pick the right man early, set your sights by him, go after him, pursue him' (she was waving her arms now, the drink slopping out of the glass) 'and make sure you got the important slow-dances with him. It was all so bloody cold. But it was damned important. He was my Northern Star – can you imagine that? I steered my frail canoe by him, paddled towards him as if he were home itself. My God!'

She is about to cry, the sloppy crying induced by alcohol and grief. 'O my God!' she says again, and looks around, frantic for something she cannot find. I hand her a Kleenex. Footsteps in the hallway.

She wipes her nose and Roy is fumbling the key in the tiny latch. The door opens clumsily, as if pushed and pulled at once, and I am standing with a new cigarette in my hand and no drink when Roy comes home. He too has his Northern Star. He sees me, grins, extracts the key from the lock. He is drunk, how he drove is a mystery, and he is dishevelled, his collar undone and his tie tightened into an impossible knot a foot from his Adam's apple. He searches his pocket for something, closes the door behind him, stands wide-legged in front of me and grins and holds up a bottle of Johnny Walker and salutes me. I am overcome by a weighty sadness and I remember, clear as day, the freshness of the three of us in the days of our glory, before anything at all anywhere went wrong. Days before bombs, those good old days. I look at him and he grins at me, his hair uncombed, his mouth twisted in a moronic grin. I think, oddly, of the face my wife used to make – still does, occasionally – when the rising heat of lovemaking drowns her. I see that look come over her face and I drown too.

'Old friends are best!'

'I'm just going, Roy. Glad you're home safe. You shouldn't drive.'

I step towards the door, I pull my jacket-collar up tight around my neck. Roy holds up the hand holding the bottle. 'Drink!'

'No, Roy, I've had one. Maybe more than one, come to that, and I have to drive too.'

Now he puts on the sly-devil conspiracy grin – does he use it with judges too? – as if we had, both of us, arranged to meet here in this apartment. He winks hideously at his wife, who stands motionlessly behind me, looking at the carpet. He puts a drunk's arm around my shoulders. The smell of his breath is stifling.

'To old friends, Robbie. You and I. You and I and *her* there. Look at her. She's half-pissed as well. Have a drink for me.'

His Belfast syllables seem to crush the life out of me, I had forgotten how hard the accent could be, how sharp at the edges, how penetrating. It contained a dialect constructed primarily for use as a verbal weapon. It managed to joke offensively and make everyone laugh. Roy was capable of using it to horrendous effect. There was the humour of the knife in his voice. Suddenly he removes his arm from my shoulders. He steps into the room. She steps back. Roy turns awkwardly and looks at me. He looks straight into my eyes and I stare back. Now, I think, he will hit me or hit her. I don't, God help me, know what to do,.

'I'm off, Roy. Janet, I'll see you both again. Take care.'

I'm at the door. Roy grabs my arm. He brings his face close to mine and I see how much he's aged, how terribly damaged he is, how deep the wound is. He holds the bottle within inches of my eyes and shakes it as if to make sure it is still alive. He is almost whispering.

'I *need* this, Robbie. You don't *understand*. Neither does *she*. I don't sleep very well. It's not so bad if you can sleep. You don't understand *either*.'

He is looking into my eyes again, from a very long way off. Janet is moving towards us and I see in *her* eyes the panic of a sailor caught up in a fire at sea. The Northern Star is obscured by the smoke.

'Robbie's tired, Roy. Let the man go home to his bed. And it's time you were in your own.'

Drunk enough, all refinement, all carefully-nurtured attitudes and elocutions disappear, and Janet returns to the anxious vowellings and assonances of her native County Antrim. She is a mother tending a sick child, ushering another sick one home. The refinements and the parlours came late in her development, when the seed of small houses and big sloping fields was already sown. Janet's boy-next-door would have been a shy trusting farmer's son. Roy waves her back.

'We're still old friends, Robbie, aren't we? All three of us. Maybe four, if that lovely wee woman of yours was here still.'

'I'm definitely going home now, Roy.'

'Aye!'

He turns away from me, breaking his stare, and Janet settles him back on the settee. He slops some whiskey into his mouth and looks from Janet to me and back to Janet. He narrows his eyes and looks at her. Perhaps he notices the black eye. He looks at me.

'Just give me a cigarette somebody. A fag, any brand.'

I light his cigarette – Janet's Dunhill – and watch him take deep breaths, inhaling the smoke, never setting the bottle down for an instant. I don't want to leave them together like this. I don't want to leave her here with him. But this has happened before and I have played powerless witness to it all before. And, as before, my overwhelming desire at this point is to go home to bed. Roy looks up at me, a destroyed figure of a man, everything about him folding in on itself to nothingness. He points at me with the Dunhill.

'I've always said this was *your* country. Haven't I always said so, Janet? Aye. *Your* country, not mine, and not hers.'

'This is beneath you, Roy. You're drunk and that nonsense is not you.'

But it *is*, a voice insists; this is Roy, this is his Belfast speaking. This is the voice of friendship whittled down to defeat and terror.

'I've *always* said so. But she doesn't *believe* me. She defends *you*.'

I look at Janet and she looks away. Have I been the subject of their arguments, the cause of her black eyes?

'I don't think I understand any of this, Janet,' I say, 'and I don't think I want to. I'm going.'

'He doesn't know what he's saying, Robbie.'

Janet goes to her husband's side and places two loving hands upon his shoulders. She has left down the glass. Her compass points due North again, true, accurate as always. I know that she will defend him to the end. That our friendship may very well go down under the weight of that defence. I am thinking of Yvonne, of Spain, of what Janet has told me about Roy's impotence; and I am thinking of how much I love my dull routine, how much I am at home here, and how little natives can do for exiles in the long run. Nothing can bridge the gap between us; the car-bomb blew us apart. Everything was real after that. Absurd blind prejudices, gently held in check by a devil-may-care comradeship of young drunken achievers in a city under siege, had been blown all over the road. For Roy, nothing would ever replace being a successful *Belfast* solicitor in *Belfast*; the city of rugby matches, school ties, fife-and-drum and absolute certainties. He is too terrified to return there. And he hates that terror.

'I know well enough what I'm saying,' Roy mumbles. But he is out of reach of his deepest angers. I open the door. The air in the hallway seems cleaner. I hear Roy's parting words to me as I close the door behind me, and I know that this time it's all over with us.

'You're our pet *Fenian*, Robbie. No home should be without one.'

I get into my car and it begins to rain, the drizzling half mist of the Atlantic coast. No moon now, no stars to guide the helpless mariner. I am thinking only of Yvonne as I drive away from the block of expensive apartments overlooking the bay. I no longer care about Janet, about Roy, about anything we ever had. I have been cleansed, in some odd sort of way. In the good old days, if they ever existed, if we didn't just make them up, Janet had a favourite song. It was current at the time in the flats around the university, in the single rooms, in intimate nights of bottled beer and marijuana and Civil Rights. It had the lines:

> I'll be as constant as the Northern Star –
> Constant in the darkness, where's that at?
> If you want me I'll be in the bar…

Joni Mitchell. The record would stay on the player for hours as one by one, like stars, we faded out.

Gone

It was raining. Heavy, noisy drops splashed and knocked against the single long, many-paned window. Outside, the green tended gardens looked damp and dull. A low grey sky fell over the city, over the heavy-leafed trees of the driveway, draped itself over the shiny black slates of the hospital roof.

The cassette recorder was on now, the reels turning soundlessly. He was on his feet, looking out of the window. He looked at nothing, or at something no one else could see. The tweed jacket had worn leather patches on the elbows. One threatened to detach itself altogether. His grey hair was thin, his scalp red underneath it. He would move his restless hands from the pockets of his jacket to the pockets of his casual, sharply-ironed slacks, a constant, slightly unnerving action, as if he was looking for something he could never find. His voice was deep, a little ragged from too many cigarettes. The room was full of smoke, and after a period of moving his hands about, he'd light up a cigarette.

Funny, he said. All that attention all those years back. I could have done without it, God knows. Then utter silence. Then you turn up, wanting to hear it all over again.

There was a part of me, a rather large part, if I were honest, that objected to interviewing Howard. So many years had passed, his tribulations had been many and difficult. The media of the day had loved every minute of it; they had labelled him a dabbler, a lunatic, a dangerous quack, any number of things. He hadn't sued once. Even when the attacks had become quite outrageous and personal. It wasn't Howard's way. Or perhaps he just hadn't had the strength. So I felt not entirely right with myself being there, making him talk, or allowing him to; but his story was a good one, and it roused the enthusiasm of an otherwise indifferent editor. A series of articles on great medical mysteries. Howard was unavoidable.

You're young, he said, still staring out of the wet window. I'm not being patronising, do forgive me. I mean simply that when one is young one believes everything is possible. One does not believe, for example, in death. One may live forever, if one wants to. I was like that. Or something close to it.

In fact they had hailed him as a genius, another Jung. No limits to what he might achieve. I had read the medical journals, the psychiatric reference books. At thirty, head of this very hospital. It dawned on me that Howard had spent virtually all of his adult life within these walls. As had many of his patients. It was not a comfortable thought. Then had come ridicule, suspicion, disgrace which was more or less diluted by his being asked to resign and take a much-reduced position, limited patient work, yet still a hospital psychiatrist. Howard, being a doctor, had accepted. Psychiatry was his life. And perhaps, after all the adverse publicity, he feared the almighty wilderness beyond the hospital walls. As indeed, did many of his patients fear it, too.

Howard the genius, the young doctor of remarkable enthusiasm, energy, focus. He could confer enthusiasm on his colleagues; there was no hint, throughout his many severe trials, that anything was being done to him from someone's sense of envy at what he was and what he had managed to do in the several fields of mental illness in which he took an interest. Then he had become an irredeemable embarrassment. I had read the newspaper reports but I, like those medical potentates who stood in judgement on him, found his explanations incredible. Howard, when it was all more or less over, had a breakdown. Not terribly severe, by all accounts, but severe enough to warrant mention in a couple of newspapers. So, he had been unbalanced after all. That explained it, then. Howard vanished from the public gaze.

A frighteningly white bust of Schubert sat on Howard's untidy desk. Without turning round Howard asked me whether I liked Schubert. I said I wasn't quite sure. I hadn't heard much of him. Young women probably don't go for Schubert any more, Howard said. My wife used to think he was very romantic. Schumann described him as 'heavenly'. Schumann, of course, had problems of his own.

A sudden burst of wind and rain rattled the window. Howard had conjured ghosts, and they pushed and heaved to get in. She died, my wife, Howard said. I loved her very much.

Someone knocked at the heavy grainy door. Come in, said Howard, raising his voice, in command. A young nurse came in with a pot of tea, two mugs, some flat biscuits on a chipped plate, everything balanced nervously on a wood-and-wicker tray, the sort patients make in occupational therapy classes, or whatever they are called these days. Howard thanked her, smiled at her. He had been a handsome man, still was in many ways. He had bright eyes and a solid, determined chin. Frail-looking now, as a younger man he must have caused a bit of eye-turning when he entered a room. Female students would have adored him. A student when I first met her, my wife, said Howard. I was beginning to feel that, at some point in his life-long searches and rummagings in the lucky-dip of the human mind, Howard had learned how to read one's thoughts. But that's nostalgia, he said, pouring tea. We never had children and that's nostalgia too. Underestimated, nostalgia is, to my mind. It creates poems, great music, paintings, novels. Yet we ridicule it. Sugar?

I turned off the recorder. We sipped in an uneasy silence, weighted by the slow thrumming of rain outside and the heavy dark shadowy tone of the room. Bookcases, magazines on a pile in a corner, a littered and vanquished desk, a tall lamp in another corner, switched on now almost at the middle of the day, casting a shaded, wary yellow light. Howard finished his tea and a biscuit which he had held at the very point of finger and thumb. Then he started to wander around the room, asked me to turn the recorder on again and, without any further digression, he told me his story.

You'll have done your homework, I expect. You will be aware that, in my time, some very flattering things were said about me. And about my work. I was compared, erroneously, but no doubt with good intention, to various heroes of our profession.

Howard's voice seemed to have a soothing effect on the elements; the rain eased off, the wind died down. When I glanced out of the window, the sky seemed lighter, the clouds higher. Howard moved from one side of the room to the other, hands in and out of pockets, listening for his memories.

To make a long story short, then, I instituted – horrible word! – I *introduced* the notion that, by permitting some of my patients to regress, under proper supervision, to a point in their lives which meant something to them, which was crucial to them, I could, as it were, assist them to rebuild their lives from that point.

The rain stopped altogether. A frail white light invaded the room, watering down the yellow light from the lamp. Howard switched it off, barely losing his stride.

I was not interested in having them return to a point at which they had been traumatised. Nor did I wish that they should become children and play with train sets and dolls' houses. We each of us have a place, a day, a person, to which we would return if we could. A day of happiness, if you wish to call it that. A person, for that matter, who generated happiness, security. A day when we felt the world was on our side. More to the point, when we felt a sort of union with things. A harmony. If all of this sounds simplistic, I'm afraid I can't help that. It is simple. But psychiatry back then, as now with every branch of medicine, was a battleground where very old and ridiculous wars were fought. Freud-versus-Jung was still the big tournament in my day.

The bust of Schubert began to glow. Whiter and whiter it became, until it reached a luminosity which did not belong to plaster or any kind of stone. Absurdly, I wondered whether Howard had installed a light within it. Of course he hadn't.

At first, my ideas were considered irrational, to say the least. In the end, as you know, I'd be called a lunatic for them. But irrationality could be argued. I worked, with some encouraging results, with three or four very depressed patients. They'd recall a trip to the seaside, a visit from a favourite aunt. They'd smile, try to intensify the recollections, be encouraged to. They'd come back a few days later: Do you know, Doctor, they'd say; I've just remembered something else. All very basic stuff at that point. But gradually, over a painfully long period of time, a couple of them began to reassess, to *resee*, their lives, re-live them, to some degree. They rebuilt themselves and their memories, replacing bad ones with good ones, or at least reducing the effects of those that had injured them by heavy doses of half-decent, if admittedly often heavily nostalgic, memories.

A helicopter puttered noisily over the hospital grounds, high up, a flimsy insect. Howard looked up at the ceiling. Contrary to what most people expect of places like this, he said, our patients are pathetic, subdued creatures for the most part, not at all the sort that have to undergo chemical or physical restraint. I shudder to think how anyone can attempt to undo the sort of trauma people experience in our city these days. How, in the midst of terror, do you tell someone not to be afraid?

Howard lit a cigarette, began smoking deeply, inhaling the smoke into his lungs as if he were drowning and the smoke were fresh air. The helicopter moved off. I have never been able to rid myself of the feeling that I am being watched, perhaps photographed, when that damn thing hovers over me.

He hesitated for a moment, inhaled again.

Of course, my work was somewhat more complex than I am describing; it was not happy tearful memories and Granny's lollipops. But I watched some people get better, adjust to themselves. I wrote about it and received letters from colleagues who were doing similar work or who were interested in what I was doing. In turn, journals wrote about me. That was silly, the work was not anywhere near proven or finished. But, at a sort of snail's pace, I was reaching a conclusion, which is about the best of it. No patient, let's say, had actually got *worse* as a result of what I was at. Then I met the one that caused all the trouble. Let's call him G.

The catch in Howard's voice made me sit up. The memories were painful, loaded. The patient he was referring to had been named in the newspapers as William John Graham, a forty-eight year-old unmarried bank clerk. If Howard wanted to call him G, that was fine with me.

Unfair to me to suggest G caused trouble, as it were. He didn't. Not intentionally. He was following doctor's orders, after all, was he not? Taking his medicine, and all that. Well, what does it matter? I'm resentful of him. I admit it. I wish I had never met him. I sometimes wonder whether, in fact, I *did*.

A bell rang somewhere down the corridor and a woman's voice could be heard calling abruptly; an order, a plea. Then came the very distant sound of someone whistling *The Londonderry Air.*

He'd been standing outside a shop when he started screaming, Howard continued. A middle-aged man – working all his adult life, or as much of it that mattered, behind a grille in a bank here in the city – suddenly stands outside a shop in the middle of town, not just any shop, a schools' outfitters, and starts screaming at the sky. Sedated by the time he got to me. No choice. School uniforms – first thought was that he'd had some sort of dark sexual fantasy going which got too much for him. Guilt, fear, catching up. But I sat with him, watched him as he lay there in his bed. Some things, even in this profession, you know by instinct. I'd read his medical history, of course, what there was of it. Nothing weird or wonderful. Nothing with the boys in blue, either. Boys *in green*, I suppose I should say, up here. Funny thing, ironic, that; police uniforms being green in our true-blue neck of the wood. Anyway, Mr G did not have any unusual tastes of any type, let's just get that out of the road.

He stubbed out his cigarette and promptly set fire to another. He stared at it for a long time before putting it in his mouth. Wouldn't say a word for weeks, said Howard; then I put a cigarette between his lips, highly unorthodox and not approved, and saw that he dragged at it. Probably nervous reaction, but it meant he was alive and enjoyed a smoke. I'm sorry, is my smoking bothering you? I never even thought to ask. I've lost my manners, I'm afraid.

Howard flustered. I said it was fine, I smoked now and then too. Which was a lie. That's a little fib, said Howard. I smiled. I'd forgotten Howard could see into my skull. Howard smoked on.

I sat with G for days, nights. In some instances, it was later said that my other patients suffered a certain amount of neglect. I don't recall that they did. Not intentionally, certainly. I'd never have allowed that and I prided myself on a sense of discipline. But I must admit, G intrigued me. I interviewed, off the record, the people who worked in the shop. They remembered G's screaming but had never seen him before that day. Inside the shop or slavering in through the window, nothing like that. I played amateur dick for a time, spoke to people I shouldn't have, dabbled in the unethical maybe, but I had a craving to know G. My wife told me I was doing dangerous things. We never listen to those who love us. There is a certain emotional distance for listening and if someone is too close we can't hear them. A friend tells you over a drink that the lump on your neck should be seen by someone and you do it right away; your wife or husband or whatever tells you the same thing and you tell them not to be ridiculous. To do with childish notions of being assertive, dominant, I suppose. Anyway, I didn't listen to her; that is, I didn't hear her. I did what I wanted to do.

I noticed that Howard had no photograph of his wife on his desk; or anywhere else in the room. Dead, her absence was in itself a presence, as if she were a ghost he could conjure up rather than a mere memory. He didn't require an icon of her. I looked at Howard pacing about, smoking deeply, and wondered about his wife, what she'd been like for him. How no one is the same person seen from two different points on the emotional compass. How much he must have loved her, I thought, no longer to be able even to imagine her as a face smiling out of a frame.

I drove to where G lived, Howard went on. A floundering housing estate, neat gardens and too many children all over the place and a couple of high-rise blocks of flats. Hideous. Drive anyone mad. Behind it were some rolling hills, so far untouched. One looked at them and felt relieved. The estate was expanding, growing, swallowing things up. You could hear the machines coughing and barking like old angry men from G's front garden. A mile away, you could still hear them. Terrifying.

And so, Howard went on, I learned about our friend, Mister G. I looked at his maddeningly ordered architecture, which might have stood for the architecture of his inner life up to the point where he'd started screaming his head off. Frankly, I began to wonder why whole armies of people who surrounded themselves with similar sorts of order hadn't gone mad with him. Order demands a price, you know. I don't suppose you're aware of that, at your age. Think you'll plop order on top of the lovable chaos you live in, just like an old woman might wear her most respectable hat. Order isn't like that. Order is holding on tight, painfully, in utter daily dread.

For a moment Howard was no longer talking about Graham. He was off somewhere else, speculating, revealing bits and pieces of himself which I suppose he wished me to pick up. The recorder wound on and on, absorbing everything, making no distinction between the relevant and the irrelevant, and I felt sleepy. I wanted Howard to tell me more about Graham, not ramble on about himself. If Graham's story and Howard's intertwined at some stage, well and good, it was all on tape, now, chaos transmuted into a sort of order.

Weeks passed, said Howard. He was leaning against the side of his desk, a cigarette in the fingers of one hand, the fingers of the other caressing the strangely glowing white bust of Schubert. G made the predictable and quite welcome progress. He got up, ate communally, smoked, read magazines; God knows they were pretty bad ones in those days, out of date, stupefyingly unconcerned with the present. How anyone could bother with them. Thing is, he never said a word. For weeks. Not a word. Now and then he'd smile at something. Never revealed what. I had private sessions with him and he took part in group discussions. I say *took part*, I mean he was there, he sat with us, but he didn't open his mouth. And at times the bugger'd look so unreasonably smug. I felt he mocked me, quite frankly, and I didn't like that. I had urges, barely controlled, to slap the grin off his face. Wasn't a grin, really, more a sort of grimace. But I took exception to it. It offended me. It made me feel that he was unreachable, possessor of some sort of secret. To be straight, G's demeanour sometimes made me think he was having us all on.

Suddenly a shaft of sunlight broke in through the drying window. It shocked us both. We looked at it and the shapes it made on the desk, the carpet. Then it went out again. We glanced at one another. Howard smiled. The sun makes fools of us all, he said. He cleared his throat before continuing.

I had explained how I worked, he knew about it if he was capable of hearing me at all, I talked about nothing else and worked through no other topic in my group sessions. I thought to myself that, if he's playing the cod here, I'll trip him sooner or later. Matter of time. The thought was, I began to realise, a dishonourable one. I wanted him to be so sick that he obviously looked forward to seeing me, depended on me, like the rest of them did. But, though he moved about with us, ate and took a crap with the best of them, he seemed to move in a satisfying world of his own. It made me think of all sorts of schizoid possibilities. Was he withdrawn or just pissing about? Why would he play-act? Bit dramatic, getting pitched into a nuthouse. Had he debts? Had he murdered somebody? Bodies of nubile young girls tucked neatly under his crisply mown front lawn? I'd swing from suspecting him of great fraud in order to cover up some terrible crime, to feeling sorry for a man who couldn't grin but could only give a sort of toothache smile. Fields, he said one day during a group. One word in almost nine weeks. Fields. Someone had mentioned something about helping his father take in hay when he was a child. Fields, said G. He smiled – a recognisable one this time; then the grimace clouded it out. But everyone looked at him, shocked. It's a bit like that when a group patient says something for the first time; but after nine damned weeks, everyone more or less assumes that the patient's subconscious has taken a vow of silence. So old G had this trick up his sleeve, saved for last, as it were.

Howard shoved himself off the table. The bust of Schubert rocked unsteadily for a moment, then balanced itself.

My rule was to make no comment when something like that happened. You don't make a spectacle. Later, I had G all to myself in this very room. He sat more or less over there where you are. Someone needed my usual room to interview a traveller in pharmaceuticals, as I recall, bloke with a bag full of new pills to sell. Better off if he downed the lot and let us monitor the effects. In any case, G was there and I was behind my desk, not quite knowing how to begin. He did that grimace thing again and then in a voice at least as lucid, probably more so, than my own, he asked to be taken home.

Howard chuckled at the memory. G had shocked him. It was fun again. He offered G a cigarette and watched him light it himself with Howard's own lighter. Howard had handed it to him. Made him feel responsible, he said.

I took the view that G could choose to light my hair with it or his cigarette, either way would tell me something direct about his condition. He handed the thing back to me like the perfect gent he was.

From outside came the sound of high-pitched laughter. Howard moved to the window, looked out. He cleared his throat. Whatever he saw there seemed to satisfy him. He turned away from the window and the laughter ceased abruptly.

We might have been about to have a snifter of brandy each, Howard said, diving back into his narrative. Two old dons, or something. I decided it would be a good idea to enter into the spirit, as it were; one never knows, a patient may have more answers than his physician. I think I looked him up and down for a while, watched how elegantly, damn him, he held his cigarette. He must have stood out like a sore bloody thumb in that bank of his. Too much for it, really. His appearance alone; G resembled what might have been termed a dandy, in another age. And as I looked at him I realised that he *was* from another age. Some people are. They can't help it and they don't, as a general rule, affect it. You know to talk with them for a time that they are not rooted in the things that root the rest of us. G was elegant, a redundant word these days; he was mannerly, he was conscientious. I trusted him.

Suddenly Howard stopped in front of me. A bit of you is like that, he said quickly, as if to make any personal comment about a woman made him acutely embarrassed. But I could not imagine Howard embarrassed in front of a woman. He looked at me, smiled, walked on. It was I who felt embarrassed.

So I said to hell with it. If that's what he wants. Small outings at first, just to get the hang of it. I asked him why he wanted to go home, did he have things he needed collected, the usual. No, he said; not to his house, he didn't want to go there. He'd show me. A little unsure all of a sudden, I took Morrow with us. Morrow's dead now. He was a male nurse. One-time rugby player, built, but kindly. A sort of childlike bouncer. He sat in the back of my car. I'd decided to plant G in the front seat. All the way home he stared out the windows as if he'd never seen the city before. There was virtually no military presence on the streets in those days, but if we passed a soldier G would stare at him with that grimace on his face. Odd. I noted it. On we went.

A trolley went clattering down the hall. Someone was whistling and I tried to catch the tune. A light was blinking on my cassette recorder; I excused myself and turned the tape. Howard sighed, leaned up against a corner of his massive bookshelves, eyeing me. Under his gaze I grew nervous. I fumbled with the tape, almost forced it back into the recorder. I felt that Howard appraised my every movement, searching out flaws, towards some sort of final assessment. Would I pass? Not long to go, I told myself. I'll be out of here. I felt oppressed, suddenly, as if the air had been sucked from the room. I cleared my throat, felt my breathing tighten and the rhythm increase. I was beginning to sweat. I switched the recorder on again and sat back in my chair and tried to relax. Do you want water? Howard asked. No, I said. But my mouth was dry. No, please continue.

We drove to where he lived, or thereabouts, said Howard. He looked at me, frowned; are you sure you're all right? It's hot in here. That's all it is, I said. Then, absurdly, I laughed. All of this is down on tape, I said; I'll feel such a fool playing it back. Why? said Howard. Why will you feel a fool? I tried to think of something to reply to that. There was nothing there, a vast and frightening emptiness, an inability to form words. Take a deep breath, Howard said. I did, and felt defeated.

For a long time the three of us sat in the car. It was hot, clammy. I opened the driver's window, let in some air. We'd let him guide us, a mile or two past his little house. There was a field with construction workers pegging out things, attaching lines, a battery of very big and bright yellow excavators and all sorts of heavy machinery. G stared at the whole lot as if they were toys in a shop window. Then he opened the door. Morrow was out after him like a shot. But he didn't run off. He stood by the door for a while. Don't forget, he was still on medication. Things must have moved in a sort of slow-motion manner to him. At any rate he smiled at me and indicated the field. I saw that it was large and ran off down a slope towards the beginning of gentle hills and ploughed farmland. Just then one of the big machines started up, shovel down like a greedy mouth, tearing at the earth. Very primal images, those machines, you can't help feeling a little uncomfortable looking at them. G just stood and stared. Then he got back into the car and we drove back here.

Howard rested himself once more against his desk. He lowered his head, seemed for a moment to inspect something on the carpeted floor. I was feeling better; he too was gathering himself. So vain, we doctors, he said in a sort of murmur; so bloody awfully vain.

Again, the motion of throwing himself off the edge of the desk; a man leaping into the unknown, a swimmer suddenly unsure of his dive, he took a quick nervous look over his shoulder.

I believed the medication I'd prescribed was probably best withdrawn at this stage. G's improvement was radical. A day or so later I heard him screaming, a terrible, anguished, lost sound it was too, like someone in the heat of an inconsolable mourning. He was standing in that corridor out there, fully dressed, a ridiculous figure in smart suit clothes, holding his head like that figure in Münch's illustration, you know the one. All I said was 'The trees look nice today', the orderly told me. She was a young country girl. She'd been carrying a couple of bloody bedpans, had thought to be friendly to G, had seen him standing there, and made this silly remark about trees. He'd gone over the top. Nothing for it but to sedate him. Then I remembered that field; it was beginning to haunt me. Of course, they'd ripped out every tree they could find in or near it. A savage, vengeful sort of act, I'd say.

A light breeze rattled the big window. A sad droplet of rain slid down the glass. Howard turned on the lamp again. The shadows of the room were comforting.

I knew I was taking risks, but the field was some sort of key. I took G back there, put him back on a lowered dose of medication, left Morrow to lord it in his gangly harmlessness about the wards. We had to endure the soul-jarring noise of those machines and the ugly remarks of the workers. Two men, you see, out walking together. Not done in polite society. Such hypocrites we are. Anyway, I allowed G a little more room this time. He went off a little way across what was still green and untouched. They shouted at him. He ignored them. Couldn't hear them, I expect. He seemed to be looking for something, first on the ground, then in the air. A bit Prospero-esque, magic isle and all that. Full of noises, certainly. Then without any warning he stopped dead. He just stopped walking, one foot behind the other, and stared. At nothing. Nothing at all. Empty air. *Where the place*? That's Macbeth, isn't it? He stared and didn't move for the best part of a minute. I was marching towards him then, pills in hand. The air full of gross jokes from the labourers, the whole scene utterly Shakespearean, really. *Exuent omnes*, and all that.

The room darkened, the rain hammered at the window. I began to wonder whether Howard could conjure up the weather to suit the telling of his tale. Schubert glowed on remorselessly. The cassette recorder clicked and whispered. Howard smoked; the room was full of smoke and dark light.

He wouldn't discuss it. Grew happier, though. Queerly so, and quickly. Got cheery during the groups, too. Made jokes, inoffensive, but they cost him a good deal in perspiration, poor devil. He was delighted when someone laughed; it was usually me, everyone else was far too preoccupied with their own worlds to see anything funny in his. But about why he'd stopped in that field, what that had been all about, not a word. Not a sign. Not a clue. He grimaced when I mentioned it. It was a secret, I understood. When a patient develops a secret it could be good or bad; usually it signals a breakthrough of a sort, a card the patient wants to play if only you'll ask him nicely. In G's case it signified absolutely nothing. I took him back to the field, of course. He walked over it again, different spot this time, saw nothing. Several times we went back and each time poor old G didn't get what he was after. He'd go mute for days. *Fret.* I began to believe that G was inventing a world for himself and sometimes it didn't quite work out. Then one day he walked into this office, knocked first, of course, cheery as a Gold Cup winner, and asked to go back to the field. Asked for a fag, too. I gave him the packet. I heartily prayed that he would not come away with that devastated look on his face. He didn't. He stopped dead again at a different point in the field and started laughing. His laughter was louder than all the roaring of those ghastly machines, and the mocking of the workers there. In truth, if I may say it, he laughed like a delighted child. Then he stopped laughing, his expression darkened. He came back to me with his head down. Fretted again for days.

Howard walked as far as the window and drew something on the glass with his finger; an invisible cipher. God knows what. He seemed content with it, whatever it was, stood back a pace, admired it. The whisper of the recorder was suddenly very loud.

We kept up the visits to the field; I was prepared by then to risk the fretting afterwards, felt close to something. Hadn't a clue what. G was not another depressing case, nor, so far as I could make out, was he teetering on the edge of something more serious. No, all of that's not saying what I mean to convey. It's absolutely off the wall, but something inside me *refused* to contain G within the usual labels, the acceptable, the comfortable and comforting restraints we put on things to take the mystery and the challenge away. I could have slapped something on him, prescribed something; that really would have been the end of it, man like him. Did I mention that he had no relatives? None alive, at any rate. I felt sorry for him. More than that. He embodied something for me; he was the living symbol of all the sorts of loneliness and alienation we can face in this life. Sounds very dramatic. But there you have it. Sometimes I looked at G, putting on his very sane face and smoking in this room, and I saw the saddest man in the world, and he was every one of us. A child, lost, making it up as he goes along, terrified, passionate, hopeless. When my wife died I felt all of those things. G was like that. An *absent* human being. When he was in this room, it was as if no one was here at all. Odd. But I suppose some people are like that. They occupy no space in time-and-space, if you know what I mean.

So I chose to believe that G was not insane, that he was lonely, and our daft trips to his favourite field continued. I can't say that I grew closer to him, that wasn't possible. He wouldn't allow it. Man of very few words, I can tell you, our G. But I yearned to know him. Silly, perhaps; but I wanted to know what made him tick, what he dreamed, what he feared. I began to believe that G had an answer of some sort, perhaps to a question no one had had the courage to ask; I wanted at times to shake him by the shoulders and *demand* that he hand over the secrets of his locked-away private universe; perhaps I wanted to join him there.

Howard's voice had risen a note or two. I cleared my throat. He came back into the room from wherever he had been in his recollecting. He smiled, embarrassed. He cost me a lot, did G, Howard said. In some ways, I can never forgive him. Do you want more tea? he asked, with exaggerated courtesy. He had become self-conscious, awkward. He was striving to rebalance himself. No, I said. As you say, Howard said, everything's on the damned tape. He laughed, rather hideously. I wanted to hear sounds from the hallway, indications that the building was not totally empty. I was ashamed to feel uncomfortable with Howard. But my heart beat faster and my hands were sticky.

Then there came what might be termed a prosperous period. We went back to the field over a period of days – the digging was more pronounced each time, the noise more horrendous, and the slagging from the labourers more intense and vulgar – and now G was bounding about the place like a let-loose rabbit, shaking hands with the thin air. Not exactly, of course. But he'd stop more frequently, smile a lot more at damn-all, move on, stop, throw back his head and laugh. Closer and closer the machines came, louder and louder. The field was being eaten up right from under our feet. Now I feared for him, I feared some sort of utterly irreversible breakdown, a relapse of some sort. I took G off all medication and nothing terrible happened; on the contrary, he grew excited when we set off for his field, hopped out of the car almost before I'd turned off the engine. He was having a bloody great time, a child, a man in reverse, *happy*. You'll come out of that field one day, my lad, I told myself, and you'll be cured and you'll tell me all about it, how you achieved it. But he never did.

The helicopter was back, hovering gracelessly over the roof of the hospital, then beating off into the distance, a pulse growing weaker. For a moment Howard looked up at the ceiling; for all I know, looked through the ceiling straight up at it. Then he looked straight at me.

Sometimes when a patient would be near a well-remembered, familiar thing, he'd tell me about it, the things it brought back. That way we'd progress, supposedly. G never told me a damned thing and that was reason enough, so my superiors told me later, to discontinue what we were at. No certainty, you see; it was reckoned that, for whatever reason, G was in control by then and not his doctor, as should have been the case. As if a doctor can control in any way someone who has taken to living in a different world, as so-called mentally ill people so often have. Their laws aren't the same as ours, you see. It's not a question of *ill* or *not* ill. We can at best endeavour to understand that world, even enter it for a time; but the patient stamps the passport, do you see? It's not up to us. But G wasn't admitting me to anything. Then one day he appeared particularly sullen. It was at a group session. He was grimacing at nothing again. When he looked at me he lowered his head as a chastised child might do. Had he done something naughty? No, as a matter of fact. He hadn't. That day we went to the field. It had been raining, the field was ploughed up, ugly, ravaged. The diggers were silent for a moment. He walked off about a hundred yards. I watched him go, lit a cigarette. The sun came up. I remember that it made the brutish earth-diggers beautiful, shiny and glowing in the newly-washed light. The air seemed cleansed, more transparent. I threw my cigarette away for some reason. A couple of labourers moved around the field, looked at us, said nothing. Extraordinary, really. This sounds odd, but I felt very good. Very *well*, if you will. *Lighter.* I took in a deep breath. G was about two hundred yards away, now, far enough, but certainly no farther than usual. He'd made a couple of stops, a few stares. I knew he'd turn round any moment and head back, fretting or whatever. But I didn't seem to care, all of a sudden. I lifted up my arms and stretched. I could feel the sun on my hands, on my head, on my neck, heavy and warm and liquid. I closed my eyes, heard a bird singing somewhere. I realised I hadn't given myself room to hear a bird sing in years. Odd, trivial, very hippy and all that, I know. I looked over and there was G, his arms stretched into the air too. I let mine fall to my sides. He dropped his at the same time. Then he raised one hand and waved and disappeared.

The recorder looked fat and ugly sitting on Howard's desk. It had taken on a threatening and disturbing appearance in the rainy light of the room. A purring black animal full of secrets.

The rest, said Howard, you know, no doubt. It's medical history. No, it won't be that, they'll have dealt with it under some other heading. But it's history for me. I ran over that field a hundred times, frantic. Some workers helped me, thought I was crazy anyway. Then it all got serious and the police arrived. No hole for G to fall down, no treacherous crevasses. He had walked into the air; waved, turned, took a step, vanished. They were the facts I told the police. I couldn't make anything else up, though I gathered from time to time they'd have been much happier if I had. They dug the place up even more than it was dug already. No hidden tunnels, no ancient grave sites, nothing natural to explain it. So, when questioned for the umpteenth time, I gave them the facts. That G had waved at me, turned, taken one step or half-step into thin air and that was that. I was hauled up before everyone you could think of. The press loved

it and the 'phone never stopped ringing. My wife grew increasingly distressed, ended up one night in tears half-sure I'd done
away with the bugger. No, dear, I said, as patiently as I could;
he simply disappeared.

The rain grew louder, rapped at the window, blackened the
room. A small storm raged in the world. I glanced awkwardly at
my wristwatch. I couldn't see the tiny numerals in the gloom
and the yellow light from the lamp made the place even darker
still. I felt that the light in the room was being slowly sucked out
of it; into the grey rain, the low sky, the wet ache beyond the
window.

One can tell a story so many times, said Howard. It wore
me down, all of it. Relentless, they were, all of them; press,
boards, police. Might have done them a sight better to hire an
exorcist or a clairvoyant, maybe. You see, by this time, utterly
insane as the theory sounded even to myself, I'd formed a
notion of what had happened to G. Or where he was, to put it
another way. I believed I knew where he was. It wasn't until I
was in his house, courtesy of a detective inspector who was as
thorough as he was patronising, that my theory proved too
much for me. I saw the photographs. I saw the one that made
all the difference. The one where G's standing in the field, smiling, a ragged-looking urchin about fifteen years of age, between
another youth and a girl in a school blazer.

I need hardly add that, with a little adjustment here and
there for changes in style over the years, the blazer or ones just
like it were sold in the schools' outfitters outside which G had
begun this whole thing with his screaming. How many times
he'd passed that shop and remained unaffected, or hadn't notice
the blazers, or any of that, I do not know. Nor can I offer any
explanation why, on that day of all days, G should see the
damned thing and go mad. Mad with anguish, of course; with
grief. For that was it, you see. G was in mourning. Had been all
along. This dead-straight and scrupulous clerk had been in
mourning for years, for all anyone knew. Probably didn't realise
it himself. He'd lived a dead life. I don't suppose you could say

G had *lived* in any sense. His clerk-buddies came forward to the police and press and offered a drab and uncaring portrait of a man who did nothing, was almost invisible to them. A sad man, as I've said. I looked at the girl in the photograph. God knows where she is today. Doing God knows what. Certainly not thinking of old G. Nobody is, except you and I. What with one thing and another, I had a smallish breakdown, did what I was told, resigned my headship of this place, nursed my wife into her grave. Here I am. Talking to you. Reliving it all, to some degree.

Howard moved behind his desk and sat down in his leather chair. He was signalling an end to things. I switched off the recorder and put it in my bag. Howard looked weary and fragile in the half-light of the room. So much talking, so much recollecting, seemed to have exhausted him. Once again I felt smitten by the notion that I had forced him to speak against his will. Feeling guilty and uncomfortable, I stood up.

It's arrogance to say that the best years of our lives are in front of us, Howard said. His voice had dropped to a hard drone. It's a thing often said to the young when they are distressed about something they deem important. It's a very stupid thing to say, to my mind. It may also be completely false.

I tried to smile; he was rounding the thing off, I supposed, making light of his tale, attempting a little vague home-spun philosophy to make the whole business sound reasonable. But when he looked up at me, there was nothing light in his face. His eyes were slitted now, as if he were on the verge of falling asleep, or were bothered by sudden brightness; the room was as gloomy as ever.

I sound patronising, and don't mean to be. But you're young. There is so much ahead of you. Now I sound morbid. But the odds are that a fair share of it won't be all that pleasant. It's the human lot, and all that; there may come to you many moments when you will fervently wish that the past could be replayed, as it were. The past will look like a snug, sunlit country where everybody speaks your language, if I may paraphrase, and badly, a writer whose name escapes me right now. In any case, you'll pine for it. It will seem that all things are true there, everything in balance.

For some reason, Howard's low, solemn tones began to irritate me. I cleared my throat. I told him that, as a psychiatrist, he should know the folly of wishing for the past. He looked at me through his half-open eyes for what seemed a very long time. Supposing, he said, in the same monotone, supposing the best years of your life are actually *behind* you. Could you accept that? Could you live like that? Could you go on, as G did for so many years, simply devouring your days passionlessly? All those years, a clerk. Methodical, unswerving, doomed. The blazer in the window was a trigger. Who knows? Perhaps it was put there deliberately. We know so damned little of how the universe works; that place beyond books and theorising.

All I know is that G is better off now than when he was in his bank. Damn what I am supposed to believe as a psychiatrist. The world I understood was turned on its head. No one else accepted that. I accepted it alone. Officially, G is listed as a missing person. I am listed as the one who lost him. But I'd say he's never been so completely *found*. He had courage. I haven't got it. Not the same sort. I don't expect many of us would. You face an unalterable truth, you push open a door, walk through. No coming back. If you don't quite make it, you come to people like me. I'll slap a label on you, give you a selection, allow you to choose for yourself, a choice of pills and elixirs to go with it.

The rain had stopped again. A watery sunlight passed over the window, barely making a dent in the thick shadow of Howard's room. He looked once around his room as if to make sure it was still there. Then he opened his eyes wide, clownishly, looked at me, put his two hands palms-downwards on the top of his desk. Now and then in this game you come across something you cannot explain, for all the framed qualifications hanging on your wall, that's all I'm saying.

No, I said. You are saying much more than that. Am I? he asked, raising his eyebrows, his facial expressions now the sort of mimic you'd use to pacify a very small child. He was turning me against him, trying to get me to leave. Had he revealed too much? Did I think him insane, as the others probably had? How could he know what I believed or didn't believe; he was conscious now of all he had told me and I felt uncomfortable. He pushed himself up from his desk, shrugged his shoulders, buried his hands in the pockets of his jacket.

I never get patients like G anymore, Howard said. Nothing even vaguely interesting. They won't let me near them. Probably right, too. Has the rain stopped?

He turned away quickly and looked out of the window. I waited until he turned back to me and extended my hand. I thanked him for his time. I said I didn't know when my piece would appear, one never knew with editors, but I'd contact him. I don't care, tell you the truth, he said, and smiled. It's old hat now, not even something students hear about as gossip. I've been written off, effectively. A sort of early retirement, if you like. I'll see you to the door.

Howard stood in the big Victorian doorway. The smell of wet grass came up from the cropped green lawns. Over the trees drifted the slow hum of the city.

We have a savage city these days, Howard said. I'm glad not to be young and walking through it. Or perhaps that's unfair.

Howard hugged me. It was a loose, quick, paternal sort of thing, one arm around my shoulders. Goodbye, he said, and went back into the hall. In a moment, he had disappeared. Opened a door, vanished.